Tales of Magic and Make~believe

Adapted by Lucy Kincaid

Illustrated by

Eric Kincaid and Eric Rowe

BRIMAX BOOKS

Newmarket · England

ISBN 0 86112 200 3
© BRIMAX RIGHTS LTD 1983 All rights reserved
Published by BRIMAX BOOKS, NEWMARKET, ENGLAND 1983
Some of the stories and illustrations in this
collection appear in TALES OF MAGIC AND
ENCHANTMENT and CAST A SPELL SERIES
published by BRIMAX BOOKS
Printed in Hong Kong

CONTENTS

BIG AND LITTLE

Once upon a time Big the giant came to the king's palace, and banged on the gates. The gates fell down with a crash, and he strode into the courtyard.

"What do you want?" said the king, coming out in a hurry.

The giant was so very tall that his face seemed to be looking down at the king out of the sky. "What do I want?" said he. "That's easily said. I want a champion to try a bout of wrestling with me. If your champion can throw me, I'll go away and leave you alone. If I prove the better man, I'll kick you off your throne, and rule your kingdom myself."

The king who was rather old and fat, and so couldn't think of wrestling with the giant himself, snuffled and shed a few tears.

"Then I shall have to lose my kingdom!" wailed the king. "Oh, what a pity, what a pity!" He hurried into the castle to tell all his knights.

Sitting on a little velvet stool was Little the dwarf whom the king kept near him to make him laugh when he was sad. When he saw the king in tears, he puffed out his little chest and said, "Leave the giant to me. I'll deal with him!"

"You!" said the king, and he and his knights laughed and laughed. "Why, he could crush you with his little finger!"

"Not so," said Little. "It is I who can twist him round my little finger." He took a sponge full of water and a bag of flour, and out he strutted into the courtyard.

The giant was getting impatient. "I can't wait here all day," said he. "Has the king chosen his champion?"

"I am his champion," said Little, sticking out his chest.

The giant doubled up with laughter. He laughed so loud that all the windows in the palace rattled and a lot of glass fell out.

"Fight first, and laugh last," said Little, "if there's anything left of you to laugh with. But, before we fight, we'll have a trial of strength. You show me what you can do and I'll show you what I can do. Can you squeeze water out of a stone?"

The giant picked up a stone and squeezed it so hard between his hands that a few drops of water oozed out of it. "See that?" said he. "Is your head harder than that stone, dwarf?"

"Pooh!" said Little. He, too, picked up a stone. He squeezed the stone between his palms, and a whole stream of water ran over his hands and down onto the ground. "Is your head harder than this stone, giant?" said he.

Big the giant stared. The dwarf had the sponge in his hands as well as the stone and the water was running out of the sponge, but the giant didn't know that.

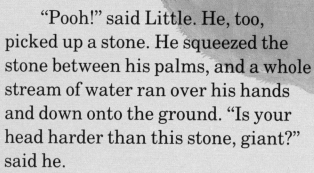

He picked up another stone and flung it onto the ground with such a crack that it crumbled to dust. "See that?" said he. "When we come to wrestle that is what your body will be like."

"Pooh!" said Little. He picked up a stone and flung it into the air, and such a cloud of white dust fell down all round him that he was completely hidden by it.

The giant stared harder than ever. He couldn't turn a stone to dust merely by flinging it into the air. Neither could the dwarf. He had thrown the bag of flour as well as the stone: but, of course, the giant didn't know that.

"You see?" said the dwarf. "So will your body be when we come to wrestle, giant, but I feel almost ashamed to wrestle with such a weakling as you!"

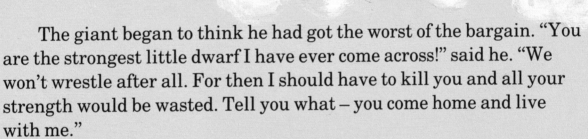

The giant began to think he had got the worst of the bargain. "You are the strongest little dwarf I have ever come across!" said he. "We won't wrestle after all. For then I should have to kill you and all your strength would be wasted. Tell you what – you come home and live with me."

"I don't mind if I do," said the dwarf. So Big the giant carried him all the way to his house.

In the giant's kitchen there was an oven as big as a barn and in the oven there were loaves of bread as big as tables. The giant put a loaf on the table, and they sat down to eat.

Now the giant was an untidy eater. He crammed his mouth so full of bread that some of it went down the wrong way.

He gave a cough and a sneeze and the sneeze made such a draught that the dwarf was blown up to the ceiling. He just managed to catch hold of a beam, and there he hung.

The giant looked up in surprise. "What are you doing up there?" he spluttered.

"Be quiet!" said the dwarf crossly. "You sneezed! If you do such a rude thing again, I shall pull out this beam and break it over your head."

"I'm very sorry," said Big the giant. "I didn't know it was rude. Come on down and – A-tish-ooo!!"

He sneezed again and this time Little was blown off the beam and whirled right through the open window. He fell on some long grass so he wasn't hurt. He picked himself up and walked back through the door.

"This is really too much!" he cried. "I can't stand such manners! I am going back to the king."

"Oh, don't do that," said the giant. "I've never met a little fellow I like as much as you and I don't want to live alone any longer."

"No, I've made up my mind," said the little dwarf. "If ever you come bothering the king again, you know what to expect. I shall throw you up in the air and bring you down turned to dust — just you see if I don't. Goodbye."

The giant stood at the door and stared after him. He felt so lonely that he wanted to cry but he went into the kitchen and drank all his wine and then he felt better.

It took the little dwarf a long time to get home but he reached the king's palace at long last.

The king was very pleased to see him and felt so grateful when he heard that the giant was never coming back. He decided that he would build the dwarf a little palace of his own with all the furniture just the right size for him. He gave him a suit of cloth of gold, and a suit of cloth of silver but the one he liked best of all was the one of green velvet trimmed with pearls. He had little page boys to wait on him, and a little carriage drawn by the smallest of small white ponies to ride out in. He had a little wife too, for the king would not rest until he found a little lady small enough to be his bride.

So Little and his wife lived together for the rest of their lives in their own little palace.

ANGRY FAIRIES

One morning Mrs Burrows the farmer's wife, took all the kitchen rugs into the garden and hung them, side by side, over the fence.

Whack! Whack! Whack! she went with the carpet beater.

Whack! Whack! Whack!

She sang merrily as she worked midst clouds of dust. She was very happy and as soon as one rug was clean she took it indoors, then came back and started on the next one.

Poor Mrs Burrows. How was she to know that the fairies had chosen that morning to sit among the flowers and chat about this and that!

The first whack she gave, made a sudden wind which straightaway blew off all the fairies' hats. They didn't like that very much. The second whack blew their hair into a tangle. They liked that even less.

The dust thrown out of the rug surrounded them in a cloud which made them all sneeze.

Atishoo! Atishoo! Atishoo! They sneezed in a chorus.

Atishoo! Atishoo! Atishoo!

"Stop! Stop!" they cried when they could speak, but Mrs Burrows who did not, indeed could not, hear the fairy voices, carried on with her work merrily.

Whack! Whack! Whack!

The fairies ran from the garden covered in dust, their eyes streaming, their hair in a tangle, their noses red, and their hats lost. Their tempers were very frayed and no wonder.

"Just you wait!" they shouted. "Just you wait! We'll be back and then you'll be sorry!"

Poor Mrs Burrows.

Back they came, that very night, bringing all their friends with them. Mrs Burrows and the farmer were asleep in bed, quite unaware that anything was wrong. Even if they had known what the fairies planned to do, they wouldn't have known how to prevent them. The fairies were going to lift the farmhouse up from its foundations and carry it to the bog where they were going to set it down in the muddiest stickiest, place they could find. That would teach the farmer's wife a lesson she would never forget when she went out next morning to milk the cows. First, they had to make the house ready to move.

They had all brought picks and shovels and wasted no time in getting to work.

Tap . . . tap . . . tapping at the mortar. Pick . . . pick . . . picking at the bricks.

The moon crept lazily across the sky. Presently they began to sing. Quietly at first, but then louder like a hundred humming bees. They worked their way all round the bottom of the house, loosening every brick and removing every nail.

Hum . . . hum . . . humming . . .

Tap . . . tap . . . tapping . . .

Pick . . . pick . . . picking . . .

17

The fairies were almost ready to lift the house and fly with it to the bog. Their humming grew more excited. The tap, tap, tapping grew quicker. The pick, pick, picking grew more insistent. Inside the house the farmer awoke. He listened.

"What's that I can hear?" he said, waking Mrs Burrows.

"You can't hear anything," she said sleepily. "Go back to sleep".

"I can hear something humming," he replied.

"It must be your ears," mumbled Mrs Burrows.

"I can hear something tapping . . ."

"It must be . . . SO CAN I!" said she, sitting up so suddenly her nightcap fell over her eyes.

Tap . . . tap . . . tap . . .

Pick . . . pick . . . pick . . .

"Probably a mouse scrambling under the roof," said the farmer drowsily.

"EEEK!" squealed his wife, who would face almost any danger, but who was terrified of mice and spiders. She dived under the blankets and hid her head.

At that moment the fairies loosened the last brick and the house was ready to lift. They threw down their picks and shovels with a mighty cheer. They unfolded their wings and prepared to hover. A hundred fairy hands slipped into the space between the house and its foundations.

They began to lift . . . upwards . . .

Inside the house everything began to shake and rock and slide.

"Whatever is happening?" cried the farmer's wife coming out from under the blankets.

"Ohhh . . ." she cried in dismay, as everything slid with a crash to the floor.

"Help!" she cried as the bed tipped over sideways. She flung her arms around the bed post and hung on to it tightly.

"What's happening? Is the world coming to an end? Is it an earthquake?" she wailed in terror.

"Of course not", said the farmer. "There must be a good reason for what is happening." Although at the time he couldn't think what it could be, when he looked towards the window and saw the stars falling to the ground.

He threw himself out of bed and crawled up the sloping floor towards the window. He caught hold of the windowsill, pulled himself up and looked outside. The ground was a lot further away than it should have been. He had never seen the top of the cow-shed from the bedroom window before and suddenly Mr Burrows was very frightened. Something very strange was happening . . . of that, he was sure.

"Heavens above" he cried. "Where are we going?"

The house was suddenly dropped to the ground with a thud! The fairies had been commanded to return to their kingdom by day-break. As the sun's rays peeped over the horizon, the fairies fled.

All the pots and pans in the kitchen jumped on their shelves and made a terrific clatter. All the plates and dishes fell off the dresser with an almighty crash.

Mrs Burrows slid UP the bed post and hit her head on the ceiling. The farmer shot upwards and then fell downwards bumping his chin on the windowsill.

Apart from one or two bruises and some broken plates there was no real damage done. The farmer and his wife never did find out what had really happened that night, or why it had happened and perhaps it was just as well.

HIDDEN MAGIC

One morning, when the mist was lying over the hills and the air was crisp and chilly, John the Ploughman took his plough from the barn and walked to a field that was overgrown with grass and tall weeds.

He enjoyed ploughing. He liked watching as the plough turned the earth and cut brown furrows that were as straight and true as lines ruled on paper with a ruler.

As the sun rose higher in the sky the mist cleared. It was going to be a fine day. John the Ploughman whistled along with the birds and was happy in his work.

He had reached the halfway mark and was turning his plough, when he thought he heard a strange sound. His ears were used to outdoor noises. Anything, even slightly unusual, caught his attention at once. He stood still and listened intently. The birds were singing in the hedgerow, the mice were scurrying in the undergrowth, the breeze was whispering in the leaves . . . but there WAS something else. It was very faint . . . but there it was again.

"I can hear someone crying," he said to a blackbird sitting on a branch.

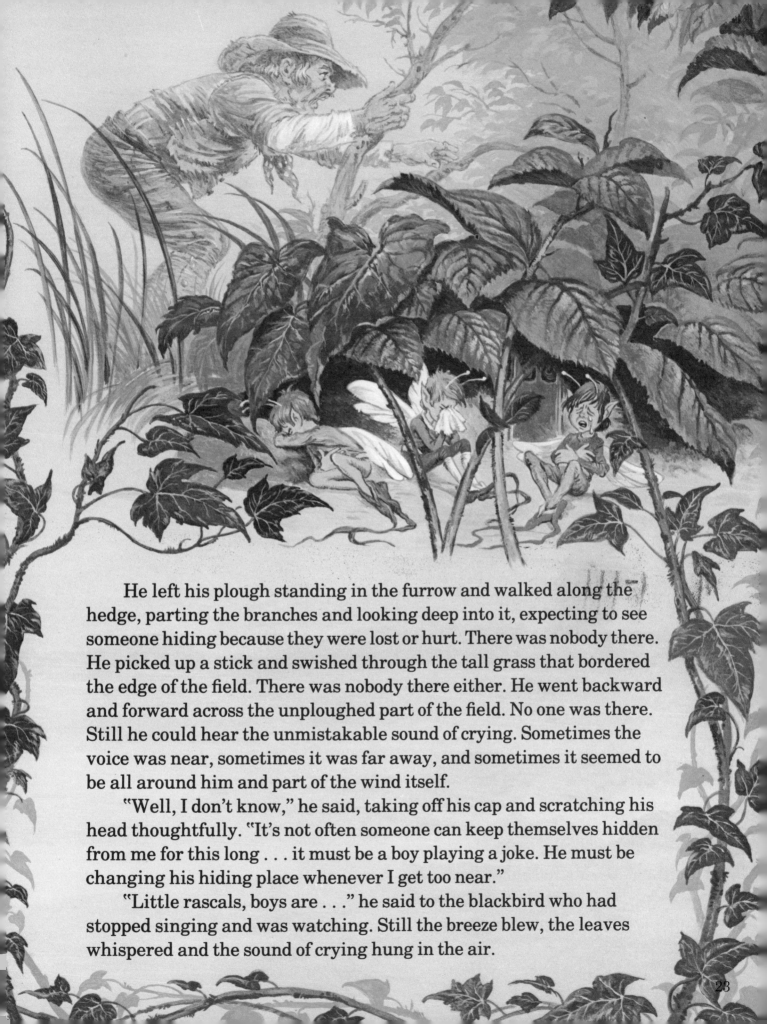

He left his plough standing in the furrow and walked along the hedge, parting the branches and looking deep into it, expecting to see someone hiding because they were lost or hurt. There was nobody there. He picked up a stick and swished through the tall grass that bordered the edge of the field. There was nobody there either. He went backward and forward across the unploughed part of the field. No one was there. Still he could hear the unmistakable sound of crying. Sometimes the voice was near, sometimes it was far away, and sometimes it seemed to be all around him and part of the wind itself.

"Well, I don't know," he said, taking off his cap and scratching his head thoughtfully. "It's not often someone can keep themselves hidden from me for this long . . . it must be a boy playing a joke. He must be changing his hiding place whenever I get too near."

"Little rascals, boys are . . ." he said to the blackbird who had stopped singing and was watching. Still the breeze blew, the leaves whispered and the sound of crying hung in the air.

John the Ploughman was about to admit that he had been beaten in a game of hide-and-seek by a boy, when he saw something lying on a flat stone close by the bottom of the hedge. It was a tiny shovel with a long handle. Picking it up carefully, John saw at once that the handle had been broken making it impossible to use.

"Ah, now I understand," said John softly. "The boy who is crying and hiding at the same time isn't playing a joke after all . . . he wants me to mend his shovel and is too shy to ask . . . boys are funny."

John cut a straight twig from the hedge with his pocket knife and stripped the bark from it. It only took him a few minutes to make it into a new handle for the shovel.

"Well," he said, when he had finished. "Are you coming to get it now that it is mended?"

Strangely the crying had stopped. He waited expectantly. But nobody came.

"I can't wait here all day. I have work to do," he said at last. "I know you are there somewhere, so I'll leave the shovel here on the stone where I found it. Perhaps you'll come and get it when I have gone." Off John went, shaking his head and thinking how sad it was for a boy to be THAT shy.

By evening the ploughing was finished. John looked with satisfaction at the neatly turned furrows.

"Looks like a bed with a brown corduroy cover," he said. "Good enough to sleep in."

25

As John walked home along the edge of the field he wondered if the boy had come back for his shovel.

"I'll go round by the hedgerow," he said. "It won't take any longer and then I'll know for sure."

When he came to the stone where he had laid the shovel he saw at once that it had gone. To his surprise, lying in the same place on the same stone, was a tiny loaf of bread.

It smelled so delicious that he couldn't resist popping it into his mouth. He could not remember ever tasting anything so marvellous before.

As John walked home, still with the taste of the bread in his mouth, he thought to himself, 'Perhaps it wasn't a boy I heard crying after all . . . perhaps . . . but no, of course it couldn't have been . . .'

But thinking about everything that had happened that day, he wondered all the same.

As well he might, for the field he had ploughed that day lay like a roof over a fairy village. The shovel he had found was used every day by the fairy baker to lift the hot bread, pies and beautiful cakes as light as thistledown out of the oven. Once the shovel was broken everyone went hungry and the crying of the children was what John had heard.

Now all was well. The children were happy and the baker was hard at work again. John still wondered about the little shovel with a long handle and the little loaf he found every Spring when he came to plough the field once more.

ICY FINGERS

Once long ago, a farmer and his wife lived on the edge of the forest. They had one daughter who was very spoilt by her mother. She sat all day by the fire, combing her long hair while the servant girl did all the work. The servant girl worked from dawn till dusk, caring for the animals and working in the fields but she never complained.

One day, the farmer's wife shouted at her, saying "I cannot bear the sight of you any longer. Go out into the fields and never come back! I will not have you here any more."

The farmer begged his wife not to be so cruel as it was wintertime and snow lay deep on the ground, but nothing would make her change her mind. Out into the cold the girl went sad and forlorn. Who could she turn to for help . . . where could she go?

She sat down under a fir tree and began to cry. Suddenly she heard a faint sound. It was Jack Frost, king of ice and snow, jumping from tree to tree, cracking his fingers as he went.

He stopped and said to her, "Do you know who I am?"

The girl trembling with cold, said in a low voice, "Yes, you are Jack Frost. Have you come to take me with you?"

"Are you warm?" he asked, as she shivered in the wind.

"Quite warm," she replied, her breath like a film of ice on her lips.

He bent over and asked her once again, "Are you warm?"

The poor girl was so cold she could just gasp, "Still warm, but very frightened."

Jack Frost was so touched by her courage that his heart melted and he could not torment her any longer. He wrapped her in warm furs and sparkling jewels and lifted her into his sledge drawn by six white horses.

Back in the farm the mother and her daughter were sitting by the fire when all of a sudden, the door flew open and there stood the servant girl, dazzling in her jewels and furs.

The farmer's wife was so angry that she said to her daughter, "Stop combing your hair. Go out into the fields, sit in the same place and maybe the same thing will happen to you."

In a little while, Jack Frost came by and found the girl sitting by a tree and said to her, "Are you warm?"

"How stupid you are," she said. "Look at my hands and feet and see how cold they are!"

Then Jack Frost was so cross that he started to question her again and again. She was so rude to him that at last, he became very angry and froze her instantly into a large icicle.

While Jack Frost was casting his spell over the girl, the door of the farm blew open and her mother was caught in an icy blast. So she too, was frozen forever.

SNOW-WHITE AND ROSE-RED

Once there was a woman who lived in a lonely cottage in the middle of a wood. She had two daughters, one called Snow-White, and the other Rose-Red. One winter evening, when they were all sitting by the fire, there was a knock at the door.

"Someone must be seeking shelter from the cold," said the woman and went to open the door.

Standing on the doorstep, his black fur sprinkled with snow, was an enormous bear. Snow-White and Rose-Red took one look at his bright shining eyes, and his powerful claws, and ran to hide.

"You look very cold," said the woman to the bear. "Please come in and warm yourself by the fire."

"Do not be afraid," said the bear when he saw the children peeping at him. "I will not harm you."

"Will you help me brush the snow from my fur?" asked the bear, as the children crept nervously from their hiding place. They picked up the broom so that they could brush him without getting too close, but the bear was so friendly and it was such fun brushing a bear with a broom they soon forgot to be afraid.

The bear came to the house and slept by the fire every night throughout the long winter. He and the children became firm friends, and no matter how roughly the children played, the bear was always very gentle.

Then one day, as summer grew near, the bear said goodbye.

"I must go and protect my treasure from the dwarfs," he said. "They stay underground in winter but in summer they get everywhere. I fear they are not to be trusted."

One day, later that summer, when Snow-White and Rose-Red
were in the wood picking wild strawberries, they saw a dwarf
themselves. He was jumping up and down in a terrible rage.
The end of his beard had caught in a crack in a fallen log and
he couldn't get it out.

"How did it happen?" asked Snow-White, as she and Rose-Red
did their best to pull him free.

"Not that it's any business of yours," grumbled the dwarf,
"but I was driving a wedge into the crack to keep it open. The
wedge popped out and the crack closed up again over my beard . . .
Ouch! Ouch! You're hurting me! Be careful!"

33

"We can't get you out on our own," said Rose-Red. "I'll go and get some help."

"I can't wait that long . . . think of something yourself," grumpled the dwarf. And so Snow-White, thinking the dwarf would be pleased, took the scissors, which she always carried in her pocket, and cut through his beard. He was free, but the tip of his beard was growing out of the log like a fuzzy white fungus. The dwarf wasn't at all pleased. He picked up the sack of gold which was lying beside the log, and stomped off, without even the hint of a thank you.

A few days later, Snow-White and Rose-Red went to the river to catch fish. Who should they see there but the very same dwarf. He was in terrible trouble. The end of his beard had caught in his fishing line, and a fish was pulling the line, and him, into the river.

"Help me! Help me!" shrieked the dwarf, holding as tightly as he could to a bunch of reeds. He was slipping all the time.

"We must do something quickly or he will drown," said Rose-Red.

Snow-White took out her scissors and snipped the end off the dwarf's beard. The dwarf fell backwards into the reeds and the fish swam away. Was the dwarf grateful? Not at all! He picked up a sack of pearls which was lying in the reeds and stomped off with a bad-tempered glare and not even a hint of a thank you.

Some time later, Snow-White and Rose-Red were crossing the heath when an eagle, which had been hovering over a rock, suddenly swooped low. There was a terrible cry. They ran to see what had happened. The eagle had its talons in the dwarf's coat and was lifting him from the ground.

"Help me!" shrieked the dwarf. Snow-White and Rose-Red caught hold of his legs and pulled . . . downwards. The eagle held on tight with his talons and pulled . . . upwards.

"You'll tear me in two!" shrieked the dwarf. But all that was torn was his coat, as the eagle continued to soar upwards and HE fell with a thud to the ground. Was he grateful at being rescued? No, he wasn't. "You should have been more careful, then you wouldn't have torn my coat," he grumbled. He picked up a sack of precious stones which was lying beside the rock and disappeared into a cave. Snow-White and Rose-Red were quite used to the dwarf's grumpy ways by now. They didn't expect a thank you. Which was just as well, because they didn't get one.

Later in the afternoon they caught the dwarf by surprise. He had emptied the sack of precious stones onto the ground and was gloating over their colours and their sparkle. He stamped his feet and shook his fists when he saw them. He was VERY annoyed.

"How DARE you spy on me!" he shouted. In the very middle of his rage an enormous black bear came ambling along the path.

The dwarf turned as pale as an uncooked pancake, and ran towards his cave. But the bear was quicker than he was and stood in his way.

"Don't eat me . . . please don't eat me!" The dwarf was shivering with fright. "You can have ALL my treasure! I'm too small and thin to eat! Eat those two wicked girls!"

The bear raised his paw and knocked the dwarf to the ground. Snow-White and Rose-Red were very frightened, but the bear called to them not to be afraid and they recognised his voice. As they ran to him, his bearskin fell to the ground. He wasn't a bear at all, but a king who had been bewitched by the dwarf, and the treasure the dwarf had been gloating over was his. Now the bad-tempered dwarf was dead, and the spell was broken.

THE WATER NIXIE

Sometimes deep in the forest, there are hidden streams where the Water Nixie lives. The Water Nixie is a sprite who likes to play tricks on children walking in the woods.

One day, a little boy and his sister, while out picking flowers, fell into just such a stream.

The Water Nixie was so pleased to have them in her power and set them both to work, cutting trees into logs and carrying heavy buckets of water. She gave them very little to eat and only cold water to drink. They were very unhappy and decided that somehow they must make their escape. They wondered how long it would be before their chance finally came.

At last, the Water Nixie decided to go out for a whole day.

"We must be quick," said the boy, but they were not quite quick enough for she came back sooner than they had expected. She was just in time to see the two children disappearing into the distance.

"Ha, ha," she laughed, not in the least bit troubled. "You think you will escape from me, do you? I'll soon have you back here where you belong. You don't really think I'm going to do the chores myself, do you?" She began to run towards the children with long, loping strides.

The children saw her coming and were very frightened. The only thing the little girl had in her pocket was a hairbrush which she threw on to the ground behind them. It turned into a hill of bristles so scratchy and so menacing it would have stopped the bravest knight.

"A hill of bristles will not stop ME!" laughed the Water Nixie, and she wriggled her way through without getting the slightest scratch.

"She's getting closer!" cried the girl. The boy took a comb from his pocket and threw that to the ground behind them. It turned into an enormous ridge of closely packed spikes, pointed and sharp as darning needles. Nothing but the wind could get between them.

"A ridge of spikes will not stop ME!" laughed the Water Nixie. To the children's dismay she jumped on top of the ridge. Holding out her arms to balance herself, she hopped from spike to spike with hardly a wobble.

"What did I tell you?" she shouted as she jumped down on the other side. "I'll soon have you back where you belong!"

All the children had left to defend themselves was a small mirror. They threw it to the ground behind them. It turned into a hill that was as slippery and sheer as the largest iceberg.

"A hill of mirrors will never stop ME!" laughed the Water Nixie.

This time she was wrong. She slithered and she slipped and slid. She couldn't find a foothold anywhere, and everywhere she looked she saw her own reflection mocking and taunting her.

"You haven't escaped from me yet!" she cried. The Water Nixie ran home for an axe, but by the time she had returned and chopped a way through the middle of the hill the children were far ahead. It was impossible for her to catch up with them, even by the use of magic. She had to go back to doing the hard work herself and wait until another child fell into her stream.

THE DRUMMER

One evening a drummer boy was walking beside the lake when he saw three pieces of fine white linen. He took one of the pieces home with him and laid it across the foot of his bed.

That night, just as he was going to sleep, a voice said, "Drummer, give me my shift." He rubbed his eyes sleepily and saw a girl standing at the foot of his bed.

"I will, if you tell me who you are" he said.

"I am the daughter of a king. I have fallen under the spell of a witch. She lets me bathe once a day in the lake with my sisters. My sisters have gone but I cannot return until I have my shift." She picked up the piece of white linen.

"Wait!" cried the Drummer. "Before you go, tell me how I can help you."

"You can free me from the witch if you can reach the top of the glass mountain, but that is impossible. Even if you find it the sides are too steep to climb."

"Where is the glass mountain?" asked the Drummer.

"All I can tell you is that the road you must take goes through the forest where the giants live," said the girl, and then she went.

As soon as it was light, the Drummer took the road leading through the forest. He beat loudly
on his drum which roused a giant who had been lying asleep in the grass.

"What are you drumming for, you impudent boy?" demanded the giant, who didn't like being woken so rudely.

"To show the way to the thousands who follow me."

"What do they want in the forest?" asked the giant.

"To kill you, and all like you," said the Drummer.

"Don't be foolish," laughed the giant. "We giants will trample you like ants."

"We will creep on you like ants when you are asleep and hit you with steel hammers," said the Drummer.

The giant didn't like the sound of that at all. "Stop drumming," he said, "and I'll do anything you ask."

"Carry me to the glass mountain," said the Drummer.

"I can only take you part of the way," said the giant. "My two brothers will take you the rest."

The giant's second brother carried the Drummer to the foot of the glass mountain. It was three times as high as an ordinary mountain and quite impossible to climb.

"If only I was a bird," sighed the Drummer. He was sitting on a grassy hillock trying to work out what to do when he saw two men quarrelling over a saddle.

"You are stupid to quarrel over a saddle when you have no horse to put it on," he said.

"Not as stupid as you think," said the men. "Sit on this saddle and wish, and you can go wherever you want to go."

"Can you indeed!" said the Drummer. "Then let me settle your quarrel for you." He went a short distance and put a stick in the ground. When he returned he said, "Whoever reaches the stick first wins the saddle."

As soon as the men began to run the Drummer sat on the saddle and made a wish to himself.

Suddenly he was at the top of the glass mountain where there was a little house, a fishpond and a pine forest. He knocked at the door of the house. An old witch who opened it said she would give him food and a bed for the night if he would perform three tasks for her.

The Drummer's first task was to empty the pond with a thimble, and sort the fishes. He worked hard, and long, but the water in the pond never seemed to get less. Towards evening a girl came from the house and spoke to him.

"You look tired," she said. "Lay your head in my lap and sleep. When you wake your task will be done."

When the Drummer was asleep the girl twisted the ring on her finger and made a wish. The water rose from the pond in a fine mist and floated away. The fish jumped about and sorted themselves.

When the Drummer woke, the girl said, "When the old witch asks why one fish is lying by itself, throw it at her and say, 'That one is for you, old witch'."

The Drummer did exactly as the girl told him. The witch said nothing, but she looked at him very strangely.

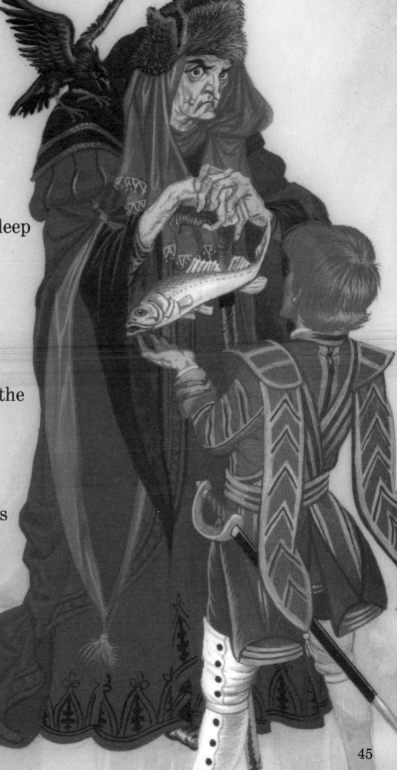

45

The Drummer's second task was to cut down all the trees in the forest and split them into logs. An impossible task, even with a sharp axe, and the axe the witch had given him was blunt.

At midday the girl came from the house, and said, "You look very tired. Lay your head in my lap and sleep."

When the Drummer woke he found the second task completed.

"When the old witch asks why one log lies apart from the others," said the girl, "give her a blow with it and say, 'That is for you old witch!'"

The Drummer did exactly as he was told. The witch looked at him very strangely, but she said nothing. The third task she set him was to pile all the logs together and burn them in one huge fire. The girl came from the house and once more told him to sleep. When he woke the flames were leaping and the logs were burning fiercely.

"You must do whatever the witch tells you to do without fear," said the girl before she went back into the house.

The witch came and watched the flames leaping and curling.

"Look," she said. "There is a log right in the middle of the fire which is not burning. Bring it to me."

The Drummer jumped, without fear, into the heart of the fire and brought out the log. As the log touched the ground it turned into the girl who had been helping him. Then he saw that she was the Princess he had come to rescue.

"You shall not have her!" screeched the witch, and leapt forward to push her into the flames, but the Drummer was quicker than the witch. It was the witch who fell into the flames, not the Princess. That was the end of the witch!

The Drummer and the Princess filled their pockets with treasure from the witch's house and went home.

"Do not kiss your parents on the right cheek when you greet them," said the Princess. "If you do, you will forget me."

In the excitement at being home the Drummer kissed his parents on both cheeks, and all memory of the Princess faded from his mind.

The Princess did not forget the Drummer. When she heard a marriage had been arranged for him she wished for a dress as golden as the sun. She took it to the palace which the Drummer had built with his share of the witch's treasure.

"What a beautiful dress," sighed the girl who was to be the Drummer's bride. "Oh, I do wish it was mine."

"I will give it to you if you will let me sit outside the Drummer's room tonight," said the Princess.

The girl wanted the dress so much she agreed, but before the Drummer went to bed that night, she gave him a sleeping potion.

During the night the Princess opened the door to the Drummer's room and called softly,

"Dear Drummer, are you awake?"

The Drummer was sleeping so soundly he did not hear her and she went sadly away.

The next day she wished for a dress as silvery as the moon, and went to the palace. The bride-to-be agreed to let the Princess spend another night outside the Drummer's room in exchange for the dress, but she made sure he drank another sleeping potion before he went to bed. Once again he slept soundly and did not hear when the Princess called.

On the third day the Princess wished for a dress that glistened like the stars. The same thing happened, but that night the Drummer did not drink the sleeping potion. When the Princess called softly, "Dear Drummer, are you awake?" he heard her. The sound of her voice was enough to restore his memory.

"You are my true bride," he said.

So, there was a change in the wedding plans. The Drummer married the Princess. As for the girl who was to have been his bride, she had the three most beautiful dresses in the world, so they all lived happily ever after.

DIGGING FOR FISH

One starry night, when the fishermen were getting their boats ready to go out to sea, an old woman hobbled along the beach towards them pulling a spindly-legged boy by the hand.

"What do you want old woman?" asked the fishermen. "Can't you see we are busy? We don't want to miss the tide."

"Take my boy with you and teach him how to fish," she said.

The fishermen took one look at the boy, who had arms like broomsticks, and laughed out load.

"You can't be serious," they guffawed. "Him. . .a fisherman! A fisherman has to battle with the sea. HE couldn't do battle with a kitten."

"Please. . ." said the boy. "I'm stronger than I look."

"Get out of our way," they said roughly. "We haven't time to waste on the likes of you."

The boy picked up one of the nets lying on the sand.

"Leave that alone!" shouted the owner and cuffed the boy's ear.

"Take the boy home old woman," jeered the fishermen. "Fishing is mens work. . .leave it to the men."

"Mens work is it!" screeched the old woman. "Well, you'll catch no fish till you bring me that!" And she pulled off the silver thimble she was wearing on her thumb and threw it onto the sand.

One of the fishermen bent to pick it up. His fingers would not close round it. It was burying itself in the sand.

It was at that awful moment the fishermen realised what they had done. They left their nets and their boats and began to dig into the sand with their hands.

"Have pity on us. . ." they pleaded. "Have pity on us. . ."

But their pleas were in vain. They are digging to this day. Their boats are neglected and falling to pieces. Their nets are tangled and rotting. All because they dared to laugh at a witch and jeer at her son.

PIXIE VISITORS

Pixies enjoy getting together and having fun. The trouble with pixies is, they always hold their parties at night when ordinary people are trying to sleep.

Once, there was a farmer and his wife. They had no one to help them on the farm and were always very tired at the end of the day. When the last chore was done they would put an extra log on the fire to keep it glowing through the night and go straight to bed.

One cold dark night, when there was frost on the hedgerow and icicles hanging from the roof, a pixie face peeped through the farmhouse window. The pixie took one look at the empty kitchen and the glowing fire and sent out a message. Before many minutes had passed the farmhouse kitchen was as crowded with pixies as a railway station is crowded with people in the rush hour.

It wouldn't have mattered if the pixies had had their fun quietly. But they didn't. Having fun to a pixie means squealing and shouting and screeching and singing. It means rattling and banging and slamming and clanking and popping. It means stamping and clapping. It means making a HULLABALOO!!! No one can sleep through it. Not even a tired farmer and his tired wife.

"Who is making all that noise?" cried the farmer's wife, sitting up in bed and pressing her hands to her ears.

"There are pixies playing in the kitchen," said the farmer who was on his hands and knees peeping through a hole in the floor.

"Then tell them to go and play somewhere else," grumbled his wife.

"I can't do that," said the farmer. And he was right! He couldn't! If he offended the pixies there was no telling what they might do. There are so many things on a farm that a pixie can make go wrong. They can curdle the milk and stop the hens laying for a start. If they are really annoyed they can make EVERYTHING go wrong.

"We'll just have to put up with the noise," sighed the farmer.

The farmhouse kitchen was warm and cosy and the pixies liked it so much they began to come EVERY night. The farmer and his wife hardly slept at all. They grew more and more tired. They just couldn't stop yawning during the day. When the farmer's wife fell asleep in the hen house and dropped all the eggs she had been collecting, the farmer decided the time had come to do something. But what? Offend the pixies and they were in trouble.

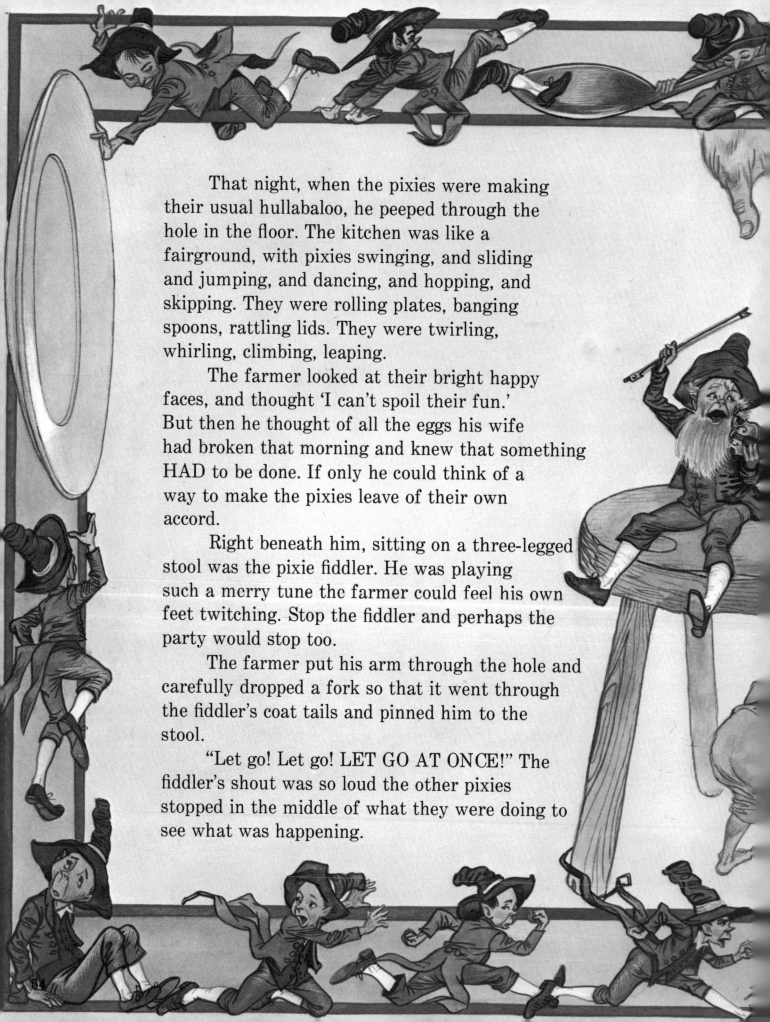

That night, when the pixies were making their usual hullabaloo, he peeped through the hole in the floor. The kitchen was like a fairground, with pixies swinging, and sliding and jumping, and dancing, and hopping, and skipping. They were rolling plates, banging spoons, rattling lids. They were twirling, whirling, climbing, leaping.

The farmer looked at their bright happy faces, and thought 'I can't spoil their fun.' But then he thought of all the eggs his wife had broken that morning and knew that something HAD to be done. If only he could think of a way to make the pixies leave of their own accord.

Right beneath him, sitting on a three-legged stool was the pixie fiddler. He was playing such a merry tune the farmer could feel his own feet twitching. Stop the fiddler and perhaps the party would stop too.

The farmer put his arm through the hole and carefully dropped a fork so that it went through the fiddler's coat tails and pinned him to the stool.

"Let go! Let go! LET GO AT ONCE!" The fiddler's shout was so loud the other pixies stopped in the middle of what they were doing to see what was happening.

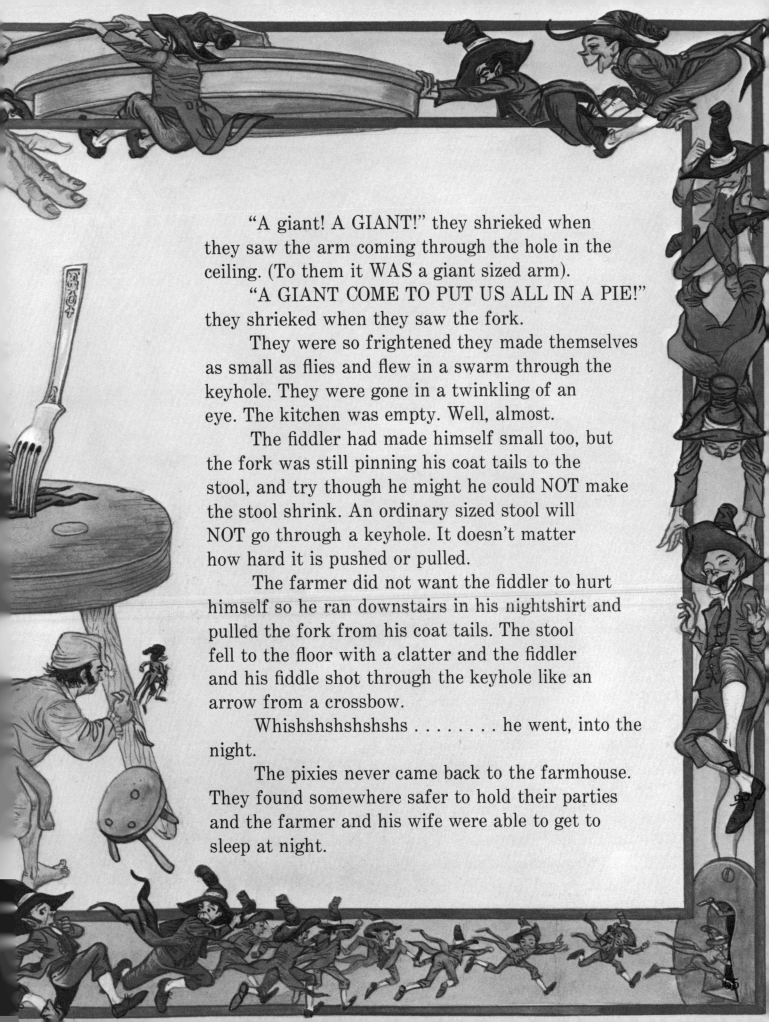

"A giant! A GIANT!" they shrieked when they saw the arm coming through the hole in the ceiling. (To them it WAS a giant sized arm).

"A GIANT COME TO PUT US ALL IN A PIE!" they shrieked when they saw the fork.

They were so frightened they made themselves as small as flies and flew in a swarm through the keyhole. They were gone in a twinkling of an eye. The kitchen was empty. Well, almost.

The fiddler had made himself small too, but the fork was still pinning his coat tails to the stool, and try though he might he could NOT make the stool shrink. An ordinary sized stool will NOT go through a keyhole. It doesn't matter how hard it is pushed or pulled.

The farmer did not want the fiddler to hurt himself so he ran downstairs in his nightshirt and pulled the fork from his coat tails. The stool fell to the floor with a clatter and the fiddler and his fiddle shot through the keyhole like an arrow from a crossbow.

Whishshshshshshs . . . . he went, into the night.

The pixies never came back to the farmhouse. They found somewhere safer to hold their parties and the farmer and his wife were able to get to sleep at night.

POET, GOBLIN AND DONKEY

Once there was a poet who could make up songs that would entice the fish from the sea, the birds from the sky, and the worms from the ground. The words he sang were as magical as any spell.

One day, the Queen's daughter fell into a sulk. The Queen sent for the poet.

"Your Majesty," he said, bowing very low. "Can I be of service?"

"The Princess woke this morning with a pimple on the end of her nose," said the Queen. "The only thing I know of that will cure it is the magic . . . "

"Oh, how kind," interrupted the poet. "How kind to say the magic of my songs will charm away a pimple and restore the Princess to her former beauty . . . "

"Don't interrupt . . . " said the Queen. "That wasn't what I was going to say at all. The only thing that will cure it in time for the ball tonight, is the magic ointment owned by the Goblin of the Rock. I command you to go and get it."

"But the goblin hasn't been seen for at least a hundred years," said the poet. "He NEVER leaves the rock."

"Then try your magic songs on him . . . " said the Queen.

It was a royal command, so the poet had to go.

The goblin was curled into a
tight ball in the very heart of
the rock. He was deaf to the
world, or so everyone thought.

The poet knew it was going
to be difficult. He knew he
would have to sing as he had
never sung before. He sang
softly with strange mysterious
words, and at last there was a
faint stirring inside the rock.
Presently the top of the goblin's
bald little head began to show.
The poet could see his forehead
. . . then two slanting eyes . . . then
a long pointed nose . . . then thin
lips . . . and a round chin. Then
two knobbly shoulders appeared.

The poet was drawing the goblin from the rock as gently and
as surely as a maiden draws a fine thread from a bundle of flax.
Now the tops of the goblin's spindly arms were showing . . . now his
bony elbows . . . now the poet could see the hand holding the precious
bowl of ointment . . .

At that precise moment a donkey brayed, right beside the poet's elbow. "EEE! AAWWW!" The poet's song had charmed HIM out of his stable, across a field, over a stream, through a wood, over a hill . . .

"EEE! AWW!" he brayed again, as though to say, "I've come!"

The poet was startled out of his wits and fell over backwards. The goblin was so frightened he shot high into the air in a tangle of arms and legs and rock dust.

Before the poet could recover his senses enough to catch him the goblin had disappeared into a new hiding place carrying the precious ointment with him.

And that's how it was that a proud princess went to a ball hiding the pimple on the end of her nose behind a fan.

It all goes to show that a poet's spell can be broken as easily as any other spell and that sometimes a poet can be too clever by half.

THE GIANT STONES

Once there was a shepherd boy who always took his sheep to graze on a high and windy plain. On a clear day he could see for miles whichever way he looked. In one direction was the village where he lived. In another was a distant winding river. And standing right in the middle of the plain, where the wind never stopped blowing, there was a circle of giant stones. No one knew how they had got there. The village people were afraid to go near them for there were tales that they were giants who had been turned into stone as a punishment. They were the only shelter the shepherd boy had when the wind blew icy cold, or the rain swept across the plain in torrents. They cast the only shadow when the sun was scorching hot. The shepherd boy was not afraid of them. He even, in time, came to look upon them as his friends.

Living in the same village as the shepherd boy was a sorcerer who could understand the language of animals and birds. One day he overheard two birds talking outside his study window.

"Have you heard . . ." one of them was twittering. "This Midsummer Eve, at midnight, the stones on the plain will rise from their pits and go to the river to drink."

"And have you heard . . ." twittered the second bird, "that there is treasure in the pits where the stones stand?"

"And have you heard . . ." said the first bird, "that if anyone takes the treasure it will turn to dust unless they give the stones a human sacrifice in return?"

The sorcerer rubbed his hands with glee, and began to plot. The treasure was his for the taking. But what could he do about the human sacrifice? The only person in the village who had no family to ask awkward questions when he disappeared was the shepherd boy. It would have to be him.

stones, he began to think differently. 'It would be very unfair to steal the stones' treasure when they are drinking and unable to protect it,' he thought. 'I will not do it. I don't care if I stay poor all my life. I will not do it.'

There was a rustling in the brambles beside him, and to his astonishment a strange child with furry ears and bright black eyes appeared.

He went in search of the shepherd boy, and after swearing him to secrecy he told him all that he had overheard. All, that is except one very important detail. He said nothing about the human sacrifice.

"We'll meet on the plain at midnight," said the sorcerer. "And when the stones go to drink we will have treasure beyond our wildest dreams . . . now remember, not a word to anyone."

At first, the shepherd boy was as excited as the sorcerer at the thought of the treasure, but later that day, as he was sitting in the shade of Old Mighty, the biggest of the seven

"You are right in what you think," said the strange child. "It would be wrong to steal from the stones, but they are your friends and give you leave to take some of their treasure. But first, you must cut a long trail of honeysuckle and lay it beside Old Mighty, and you must only take treasure from Old Mighty's pit."

On Midsummer Eve, the sorcerer and the shepherd boy went to the circle of stones and lay in wait for midnight. Just before the magic hour clouds covered the moon. Moments later the earth began to tremble. The stones were stepping from their pits. It was an awesome sight. Were they really enchanted giants? They began to move across the plain, rocking gently from side to side on invisible feet.

Presently there came the sound of a distant rumble. It grew louder. The stone giants were returning from the river.

'I must get out of this pit or I will be squashed under Old Mighty,' thought the shepherd boy and tried to climb out. The sides of the pit were slippery and steep. He couldn't find a foothold anywhere. He could hear the sorcerer screaming with fear.

"Quick!" cried the sorcerer, "We haven't got much time!"

The shepherd boy jumped into the pit from which Old Mighty had stepped. He gathered enough treasure to fill one of his pockets. In a nearby pit the sorcerer was shovelling treasure into sacks as fast as he could. And all the time he was shovelling he was thinking, 'No one will miss the shepherd boy . . . no one will miss the shepherd boy.'

The shepherd boy resigned himself to certain death. He looked up at the sky for the last time and saw the strange child with furry ears, peeping over the rim of the pit.

"Take hold of this," called the strange child, and lowered the trail of honeysuckle which the shepherd boy had cut and laid beside Old Mighty earlier in the day. "I will pull you up . . ."

It was a very close thing. As the shepherd boy fell gasping onto the grass Old Mighty stepped into the pit with a heavy thud. All around there were echoing thuds, and then, when the earth stopped trembling, complete silence. It was as though the stones had never moved.

The sorcerer was never seen again. The shepherd boy became a rich landowner, and though he never took sheep to graze on the plain again, he was often seen leaning against Old Mighty with a far-away look in his eyes.

FRENCH PUCK

French Puck was very fond of playing tricks. He never did anyone harm, but he sometimes made people feel very foolish.

One day he overheard two people talking.

"It is our wedding day a week from tomorrow," said Jeanne. "It is market day today. We must go into town and buy all the things we need to set up house."

"There will be a lot to carry," said Jules. "We must take the horse and cart."

French Puck chuckled to himself, and sat on a fence and teased some chickens to while away the time while he waited for their return. With so many things to buy they were sure to forget something.

It was late afternoon before Jeanne and Jules returned. The cart was so loaded there was barely room for them on it.

French Puck leapt through the air, light as a goose feather, and sat on a chair leg behind them.

"Have we knives?" Jeanne was asking.

"Yes."

"Have we soap?"

"Yes."

"Then we have everything we need," said Jeanne with a happy sigh, and she snuggled up to Jules and began to dream about their wedding day.

The horse was trotting. The birds were singing. Jules was whistling. Jeanne was dreaming. And French Puck was waiting. He didn't have long to wait.

Suddenly, Jeanne sat up with such a start, Jules jerked on the horse's reins, and between them they almost upset the cart.

"Oh, no," wailed Jeanne.

A gleeful grin spread across French Puck's face. He rubbed his hands together in anticipation and his pointed ears twitched.

'Ho, ho,' he thought to himself. 'She's remembered something she has forgotten.'

"Whatever made you shout out like that?" asked Jules when they had quietened the horse and made sure nothing had fallen from the cart.

"I've forgotten to buy the thread the dressmaker needs to sew my wedding clothes," sighed Jeanne.

"Is THAT all! Surely you've got thread at home," said Jules.

"Only white . . . I need pink, and the palest of yellow, and apricot and delicate sky blue, and one with a touch of green in it. We shall have to go back to town to get some."

Jules sighed. It was a long way back to town, but he supposed he would have to go. He had the cart turned half way across the road when Jeanne cried out again.

"Look! Look!"

"What now?" grumbled Jules, who had quite enough to do trying to persuade the horse to take the right direction.

"Hey! Be careful!" he cried as Jeanne jumped from the cart.

"Look! A ball of thread!" And what a ball of thread it was! It had ALL the colours in it that she needed -- pink, yellow, apricot, sky blue and delicate green.

"Oh, what a lucky thing I saw it," cried Jeanne.

"But how did it get there?" asked Jules.

"This isn't the time to be asking silly questions," said Jeanne, climbing back onto the cart.

Jules turned the cart homewards again and they continued on their way, with Jeanne carrying the precious ball of thread on her lap, and with French Puck doing somersaults on the chair leg behind them.

The dressmaker was very pleased when she saw the thread.

"It's absolutely perfect," she said. She was even more pleased with it as she sewed the wedding clothes. It was as smooth as silk, it didn't break, it didn't knot, and each colour was exactly the right length.

The wedding day came, and everyone, and that included French
Puck, gathered outside the church to see the new bride. How
pretty she looked.

"What a beautiful dress!" everybody exclaimed.

And then it happened! Crick! Crack! The tiny coloured
bows decorating the skirt began to float to the ground.

"Ooh!" gasped Jeanne.

"What is happening?" gasped everyone else.

Crick! Crack! The muslin flowers decorating the bodice
fell in a shower of petals.

Crick! Crack! The frill round the bottom of the skirt fell to the ground . . . then the skirt itself tumbled round Jeanne's ankles . . . the sleeves came apart and fell from her arms . . . the bodice fell into five different pieces.

Poor Jeanne was left standing in her petticoat, with her wedding dress in tatters around her. Someone ran from the crowd and put a cloak round her shoulders, and Jules took her home so that she could put on another dress.

"The thread I sewed with must have been rotten," said the dressmaker, who was blushing as scarlet as Jeanne herself. Oh, the shame of it all.

When everyone else had gone, she gathered the pieces together. She looked at them very carefully. She turned each piece over and over. She couldn't find one tiny piece of sewing thread anywhere. It had ALL disappeared.

"I should have known such perfect thread was too good to be true," she sighed.

The mystery was never explained, but then nobody had seen French Puck, had they?

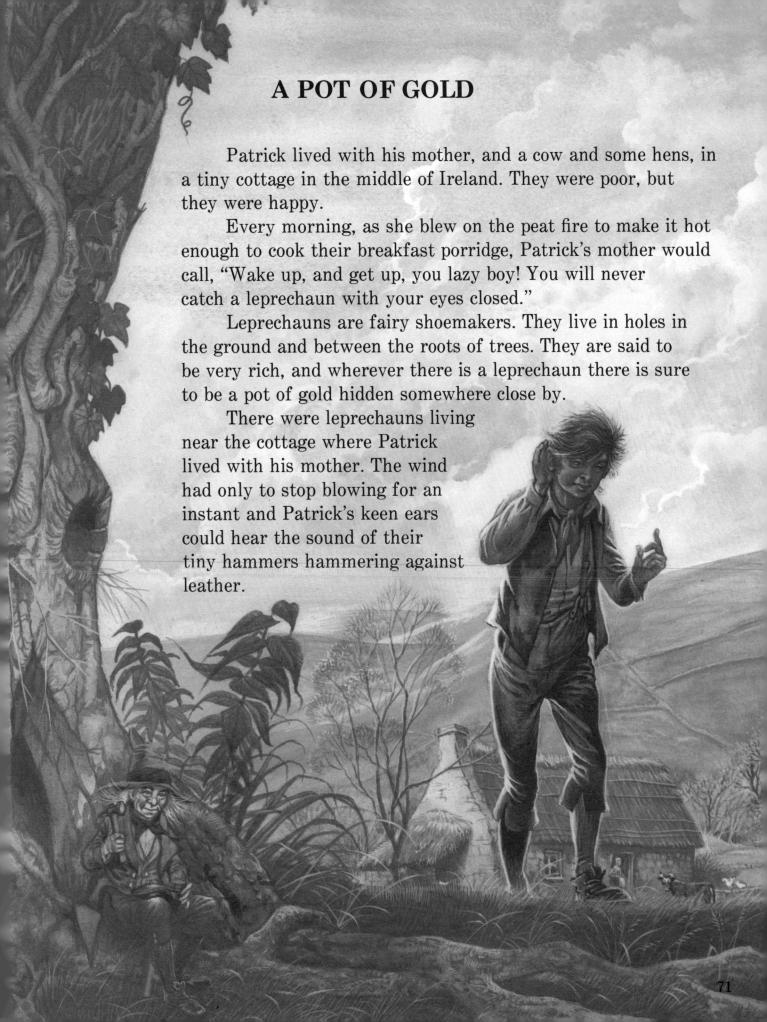

A POT OF GOLD

Patrick lived with his mother, and a cow and some hens, in a tiny cottage in the middle of Ireland. They were poor, but they were happy.

Every morning, as she blew on the peat fire to make it hot enough to cook their breakfast porridge, Patrick's mother would call, "Wake up, and get up, you lazy boy! You will never catch a leprechaun with your eyes closed."

Leprechauns are fairy shoemakers. They live in holes in the ground and between the roots of trees. They are said to be very rich, and wherever there is a leprechaun there is sure to be a pot of gold hidden somewhere close by.

There were leprechauns living near the cottage where Patrick lived with his mother. The wind had only to stop blowing for an instant and Patrick's keen ears could hear the sound of their tiny hammers hammering against leather.

It was Patrick's dearest
wish to find a pot of gold.
But first he had to find a
leprechaun to show him where
there was one hidden.

"If you happen to see a
leprechaun," said Patrick's
mother, at least once every
day, "Do not take your eyes
off him for a moment. If you do
he will disappear and then you
will never find a pot of gold."

One day, when Patrick was
returning home after another
fruitless search, he heard the
sound of tapping. He looked
down, and there, in the long
grass at his feet, was a
leprechaun. He was so busy,
hammering away at a pair of
hob-nailed boots, he hadn't
noticed Patrick.

Patrick moved very quickly.

"Got you!" he cried as he caught the leprechaun in his hand.

"Let me go! Let me go!" shouted the leprechaun, struggling to get free.

"Tell me where your gold is hidden first!"

"G.g.gold . . . " The leprechaun turned very pale.

"Yes . . . tell me . . . or I will not let you go . . . not EVER!"

"Quick! Look behind you! There's a cow in the corn!" cried the leprechaun.

Just in time, Patrick remembered NOT to look.

"Ha . . . ha . . . you don't catch me that way. I won't take my eyes off you. Now where is your pot of gold?"

"I haven't got a pot of gold . . . " cried the leprechaun. "Quick! Look behind you! Your house is burning!"

Patrick almost did look THAT time.

"You're holding me too tight," squealed the leprechaun. "You're squeezing the breath out of me!"

73

"It's no good trying to trick me," said Patrick. "I'm not letting you go until you tell me where your gold is hidden."

"I'll show you where it is," said the leprechaun.

Patrick took off his braces, tied them round the leprechaun's waist and put him on the ground.

"NOW you can show me," said Patrick, without letting go of the braces. The leprechaun led him to a field of thistles.

"It's under THAT thistle," said the leprechaun, pointing to an extra prickly one "You'll need a spade to dig it up. You had better go home and get one."

Patrick thought quickly. How could he mark the thistle so that when he returned he would know which one it was.

"I'll put my garter round it," he said, and taking off one of the garters that held up his woollen socks, he placed it over the prickly thistle.

"NOW I'll go home and get the spade," he said, "and to make sure you don't play any tricks on me I'll put you in my pocket."

Patrick ran home, got a spade and ran all the way back.
But when he reached the field, instead of digging, he sat down
and howled. He cried and he sobbed. He held his head in his
hands. Tears as big as raindrops rolled down his cheeks.
Someone – I wonder who – had put a scarlet garter round every
thistle in that field. There wasn't ONE thistle that did not
have a scarlet garter for a belt. The leprechaun had tricked
him after all. His mother had told him not to take his eyes off
the leprechaun, hadn't she, and when Patrick put the leprechaun
in his pocket that is exactly what he had done. He never saw
another leprechaun and so he never found a pot of gold. His
mother said, it was entirely his own fault.

SEEING IS BELIEVING

Once there was a wizard who sometimes left his secret room and went into the market place. He liked entertaining people with his tricks. They enjoyed it, and so did he.

"Roll up! Roll up!" he cried one day. "Come and see my magic bird!" It wasn't long before a crowd had collected.

"Come on then, show us what it can do!" shouted a boy who was carrying a plank of wood on his shoulder.

"Lend me your plank for a minute or two," said the wizard.

"It won't come to any harm, will it?" asked the boy.

"Of course not. Put it on the ground," said the wizard. He took a cockerel from a sack and put it on the ground beside the plank.

"Watch carefully," he said. He fluttered his fingers over the cockerel and chanted some strange words. To the astonishment of the crowd the cockerel lifted the plank with its beak and began to strut up and down with it.

"How can it do that?" cried the boy whose plank it was. "That's heavy. . .I know. . .I've been carrying it."

Oohs and aahs of astonishment swept through the crowd like a gust of wind.

A girl at the edge of the crowd stood on her tiptoes so that she could see better.

"What's clever about that?" she said. "Any cockerel is strong enough to pick up a straw!" The girl had a four-leaf clover in her hand and could see things exactly as they were. The wizard's magic had fooled everyone else, but it didn't fool her.

Her words were enough to break the spell, and then everyone saw that the cockerel was carrying a straw.

"Cheat! Cheat!" they shouted. The poor wizard, who had only been trying to entertain them, was pelted with cabbages and rotten tomatoes and chased out of town. How everyone laughed at his discomfort. The girl with the four-leaf clover laughed loudest of all.

The months passed, and then one day, there was a village wedding. The villagers were walking in procession across the fields, to the church where the wedding was to be held, when those behind tripped over the heels of those in front. The procession had stopped.

"What is it? What is happening?" asked the people at the back as they jostled to the front to see what was wrong.

They had come to a stream which was far too wide to jump across. There was no bridge over it, and no plank with which to make a bridge.

"We'll have to go back the way we have come, and take the long way round to the church," they cried.

"No! No, we can't do that. I'll be late for my wedding," cried the bride, who was the girl who had found the four-leaf clover.

"Then what shall we do!" they asked her.

In answer the bride kicked off her shoes. She bundled her skirt round her knees and stepped into the stream.

"Brrr . . . it's very cold," she shivered. "Ouch! It's very stony," she winced as she carefully stepped her way across.

"Do not get your wedding dress wet," called the onlookers, those that is, who were not running as fast as their legs would take them the long way round to the church. They began taking off their own shoes, and tucking up their own skirts. The men rolled up their trouser legs. Soon, everyone was wincing and shivering as they followed the bride.

"Where are your eyes that you think that is water?" asked a mocking voice.

All eyes turned towards the bank. They saw the familiar face of the wizard. All eyes looked downwards. Instead of water they were wading through grass and blue flax flowers. They were holding their shoes above their heads. They were all showing their knees. The wizard was having the last laugh, and now it was they who had the red faces. How foolish they looked and how foolish they felt.

THREE GOLDEN HAIRS

Once there was a poor man whose only son was born under a lucky star. It was foretold that, one day, he would marry the King's daughter.

The King was very cross when he heard the news. "A poor boy like that marry my daughter! NEVER!" he said. He went to see the boy's father.

"I want to buy your son," he said.

The King was told the boy was not for sale, but he nagged, and argued, and pleaded, till at last the boy's father thought, 'My son can come to no harm with the King. He will give him a better life than I can. . .I must let him go.'

The King carried the baby off. But instead of taking him home to the palace, he put him in a box and cast the box adrift on the river. With any luck it would float out to sea and the baby would never be seen again. Marry his daughter indeed!

The boy hadn't been born under a lucky star for nothing. The box was fished from the river by a miller. He took the baby home to his wife and they brought him up as their own son. He grew into a fine strong lad, full of mischief, but kind too.

One day, the King happened, just by chance, to call at the mill.

"What a handsome boy," said the King. "Is he your son?"

"Oh that he was," sighed the miller fondly. "We found him, as a baby, floating down the river in a box."

The King went pale. He called for pen and paper and quickly wrote a letter which he sealed with bright red wax.

"Can you spare the boy to carry this letter to the Queen?" he asked the miller. "It is very urgent."

"Jack will be honoured to carry your letter," said the miller, little knowing that the King had written 'Kill the bearer of this letter. Will explain when I get home.'

Jack set off immediately. Towards nightfall he knocked at a cottage door and asked for shelter for the night.

"This is the home of a band of robbers," said an old woman who answered. "Are you sure you want to stay?"

"I am carrying a letter to the Queen. They will not harm me," said Jack. He was asleep when the robbers returned so he did not see them open the letter.

"Look at this!" they said. "Now isn't that just disgraceful. Kill a nice lad like that . . . we'll soon settle this." They wrote a new letter which said, 'Marry the bearer of this letter to our daughter', and fixed the King's seal so that it looked as though it had never been broken. They burnt the letter the King had written.

81

Jack continued his journey next day without knowing that the letter had been changed. He was very pleased to marry the Princess when the Queen arranged it.

When the King returned and found he had a new son-in-law he was very angry. "If you want to stay married to my daughter you must bring me three golden hairs from the head of the giant," he thundered, thinking secretly that the giant would soon put an end to Jack.

Jack set off at once. The guard at the gate of the first city he passed through asked him if he knew why the fountain in the market place had run dry. "I will give you an answer when I return," said Jack. The guard at the gate of another city asked Jack if he knew why a tree which had once borne golden apples no longer bore even a leaf. "I will have an answer for you when I return," said Jack.

The ferryman who took him across the lake asked how he could escape from the ferryboat and gain his liberty. Once again, Jack said he would give an answer on his return.

When Jack reached the giant's cave, the giant was not at home. "What do you want from him?" asked the giant's grandmother.

"Nothing very much," said Jack boldly. "Just three golden hairs from his head."

The giant's grandmother frowned. "That could be very risky," she said. "I'd better help you. But first you must hide." She turned Jack into an ant and hid him in her apron.

While they were waiting for the giant to come home Jack asked the grandmother if she knew why the city fountain had run dry.

"I do not," she said, "But I'll ask the giant if he knows."

"Will you also ask him why the tree which used to bear golden apples bears them no longer, and what the ferryman must do to gain his liberty?" asked Jack.

"I can smell boy!" said the giant when he got home. "Where is he?" But Jack was well hidden and the giant wanted his supper so he soon gave up looking.

After he had eaten the giant lay his head in his grandmother's lap and went to sleep. It wasn't long before he was snoring.

The grandmother tweeked one of the golden hairs from the giant's head.

"What was that?" cried the giant, waking up with a start.

"Nothing dear," said the giant's grandmother. "I was dreaming of a fountain which has run dry. Why would a fountain run dry dear?"

"Because there is a toad sitting under it," said the giant who knew the answer to almost everything. "Kill the toad and the water will flow again."

As soon as the giant closed his eyes the giant's grandmother tweeked out another of his hairs.

"Ouch!" cried the giant. "What was that?"

"Nothing dear," said the giant's grandmother. "I had another dream, that was all. Now why should an apple tree that used to bear golden apples bear them no longer?"

"There is a mouse gnawing at the root. Kill the mouse and the tree will bear fruit again," yawned the giant sleepily.

The giant's grandmother thought it better to wait a while before she pulled out the third hair.

"Ouch!" said the giant when she did. "I suppose you've had another dream?"

"Yes, I have. How did you guess?" she asked. "Now tell me, what must the ferryman do to gain his liberty?"

"Give the rudder to another passenger of course," sighed the giant. "Now will you let me get some sleep?"

"Of course dear. I won't disturb you again, I promise," she said.

84

The next day, when the giant's grandmother had turned Jack into himself, he set off for home.

Jack waited until he was safely across the lake before he told the ferryman how he could gain his liberty and when he answered the questions the city guards had asked, he was richly rewarded with gold and silver.

The King had to smile and pretend to be pleased when he saw Jack, for not only had Jack brought the three hairs, he was now very rich. The Princess really was pleased to see him.

It so happened that the King himself was the next person to cross the lake. The ferryman handed him the rudder. The King is ferrying passengers to this day, which probably serves him right. Perhaps, one day, Jack will tell him what he told the ferryman.

MOLLY WHUPPIE

Once there was a poor woodcutter who found it impossible to feed all his children. One day he took the three youngest to the forest and left them there.

The children wandered, lost and hungry, until they came to a house. Molly Whuppie, who was the youngest, but by far the cleverest, knocked at the door.

"Please, will you give us something to eat?" she asked.

"Don't you know my husband is a giant and will eat YOU if he gets a chance?" said the woman who had opened the door.

"Please . . ." begged Molly Whuppie. "We are so hungry."

"Very well," said the giant's wife, and took them inside and gave them bread and milk.

When the giant came home for his supper he looked at the three strange children sitting at the table, and said, "Who are they?"

"Just three little children, very poor and thin," said his wife. "You eat your supper, I will look after them."

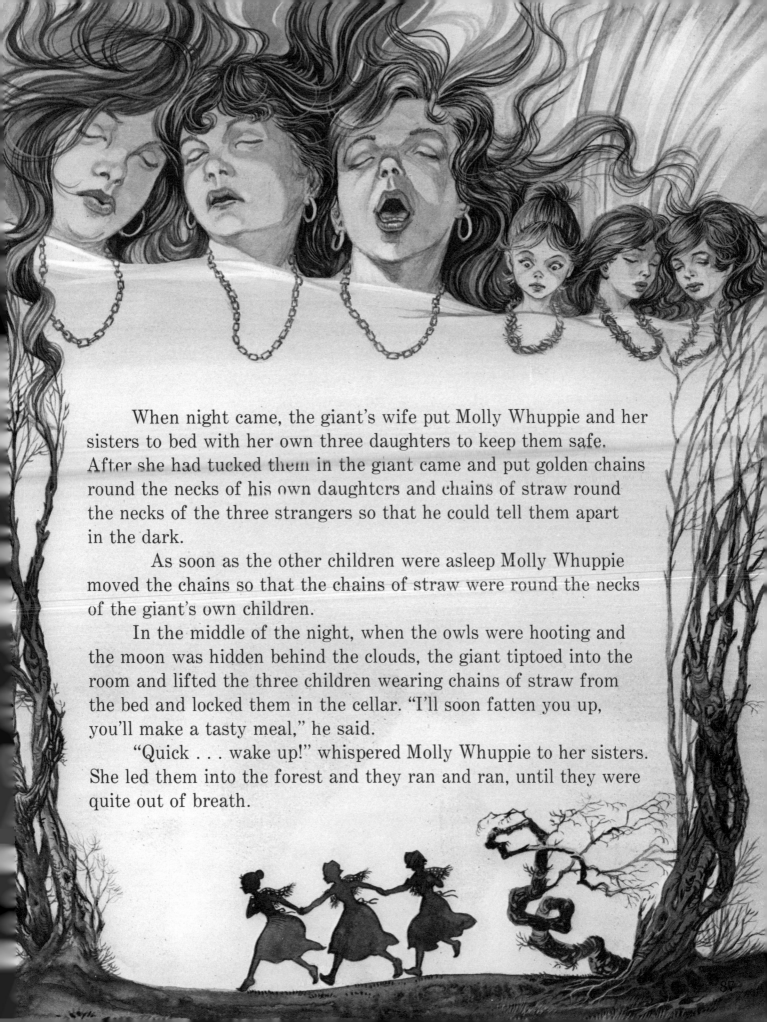

When night came, the giant's wife put Molly Whuppie and her sisters to bed with her own three daughters to keep them safe. After she had tucked them in the giant came and put golden chains round the necks of his own daughters and chains of straw round the necks of the three strangers so that he could tell them apart in the dark.

As soon as the other children were asleep Molly Whuppie moved the chains so that the chains of straw were round the necks of the giant's own children.

In the middle of the night, when the owls were hooting and the moon was hidden behind the clouds, the giant tiptoed into the room and lifted the three children wearing chains of straw from the bed and locked them in the cellar. "I'll soon fatten you up, you'll make a tasty meal," he said.

"Quick . . . wake up!" whispered Molly Whuppie to her sisters. She led them into the forest and they ran and ran, until they were quite out of breath.

Next day they came to a house that stood beside a lake, and was surrounded by statues, and beautiful gardens. It was the house of a King. He invited them in and Molly Whuppie told him how they had tricked the giant.

"Ho, ho," laughed the King. "Well done! But I know of a better trick. If you go back to the giant's house and bring me the small sword which hangs beside his bed, your eldest sister shall marry my eldest son."

Molly Whuppie had to agree, that if she could do it, that would be a very good trick indeed. That night she went back to the giant's house and hid under his bed.

When the giant was snoring loud enough to make the rafters ring, Molly Whuppie took down the sword and crept towards the door. She was almost there when the sword rattled in its scabbard.

The giant woke with a roar!
"Steal my sword, would you!"
he shouted. He jumped from the
bed with a thud that shook the
whole house and ran after Molly
Whuppie. Molly was very nimble
and very quick, she dodged in and
out of the trees until they came
to the Bridge of One Hair. And
there the giant stopped chasing
her. The Bridge of One Hair,
crossed a very deep ravine. If
the giant had put one foot on it,
the bridge would have broken and
he would have been dashed to
pieces on the rocks below.
Molly Whuppie, who was as light
as a feather, skipped over the
bridge and escaped.

When her eldest sister had been married to the King's eldest son, the King said,

"That was a good trick you played on the giant, but I know of one better. Bring me the purse which lies under the giant's pillow and your second sister shall marry my second son."

That night, Molly Whuppie hid under the giant's bed again. When the giant was snoring fit to shake the roof from the house, she slipped her hand under his pillow and pulled out the purse. She had just reached the door when a coin dropped from the purse and rolled across the floor.

The giant woke with a roar! "Steal my purse, would you!" he shouted. He jumped from the bed with a thud that shook the house so hard a brick fell from the chimney. He chased after Molly Whuppie but she reached the Bridge of One Hair before he did and skipped over it to safety.

When Molly Whuppie's second sister had married the King's second son, the King said,

"That was a good trick you played, Molly Whuppie, but I know of one better. If you bring me the ring which the giant wears on his finger YOU shall marry my youngest son." Molly Whuppie thought THAT was a very good idea indeed, so that night she went back to the giant's house for the third time.

When the giant was snoring fit to shake down a whole forest, she slipped the ring from his finger. She was just putting it into her pocket when the giant opened one eye, very, very slowly, and looked at her.

"Steal my ring would you!" he whispered, though HIS whisper was as loud as a gale, and he caught hold of her.

"Let me go . . . let me go . . ." shouted Molly Whuppie.

The giant looked at her and said, "What would YOU do to ME, if I had tricked YOU as YOU have tricked ME?"

"I would put you in a sack with a dog and a cat, and a needle and a thread, and a pair of scissors. I would hang you up against the wall. Then I would go into the wood and cut the thickest stick I could find and then I would come home and beat you." said Molly Whuppie.

"Then that is EXACTLY what I shall do to you," laughed the giant.

And he did. When he had gone into the forest to look for
the thickest stick he could find, Molly Whuppie stroked the cat
and dog who were in the sack with her, and sang out, in a loud
voice,

"Oh, if only everyone could see what I can see!"

"What can you see?" cried the giant's wife. "Whatever it
is, let me see it too."

"If you really want to," said Molly Whuppie. She took the
scissors, cut a hole in the bottom of the sack, and jumped out.

"You must get inside the sack if you want to see what I
saw," said Molly Whuppie.

The giant's wife climbed into the sack and Molly Whuppie
sewed her in.

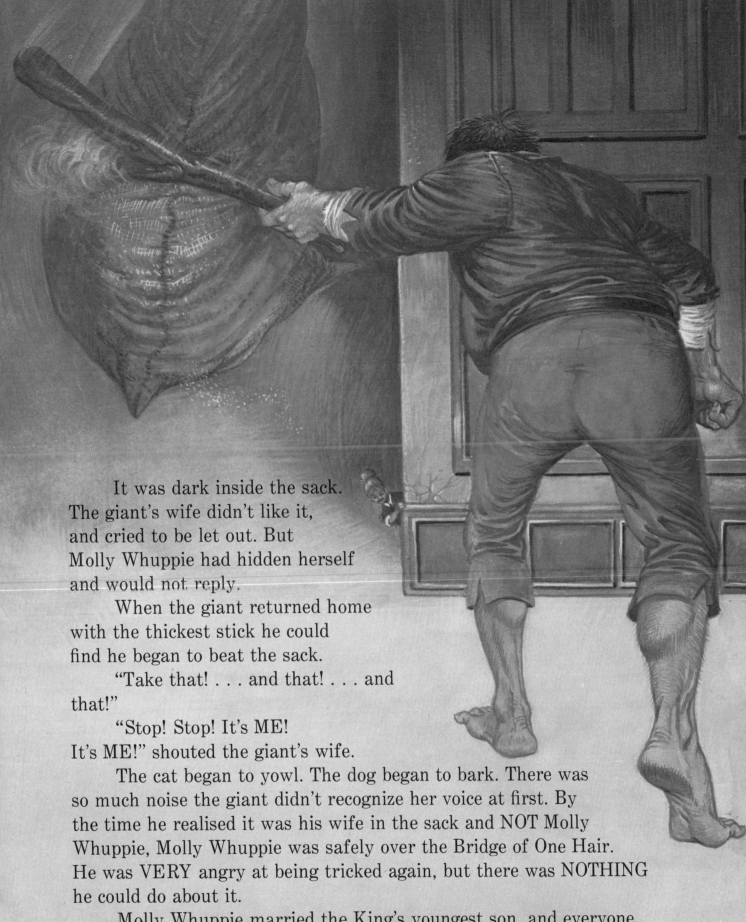

It was dark inside the sack. The giant's wife didn't like it, and cried to be let out. But Molly Whuppie had hidden herself and would not reply.

When the giant returned home with the thickest stick he could find he began to beat the sack.

"Take that! . . . and that! . . . and that!"

"Stop! Stop! It's ME! It's ME!" shouted the giant's wife.

The cat began to yowl. The dog began to bark. There was so much noise the giant didn't recognize her voice at first. By the time he realised it was his wife in the sack and NOT Molly Whuppie, Molly Whuppie was safely over the Bridge of One Hair. He was VERY angry at being tricked again, but there was NOTHING he could do about it.

Molly Whuppie married the King's youngest son, and everyone, except maybe the giant, lived happily ever after.

UNCAMA THE HUNTER

Uncama was a bold African hunter. He lived in a small village on the edge of the forest with his wife and baby son.

One harvest time, when the crops were ready to dig, a strange animal came into the village and rooted up all the vegetables in one of the vegetable patches. It came the following night. And the night after that. Each time it carried off another lot of vegetables.

"If somebody doesn't do something soon," said Uncama, "There will be nothing left, and we will all starve."

That night he lay in wait, and watched for the strange animal. If he could catch it, he would kill it. But though Uncama kept very quiet, the strange animal heard him breathing, and fled before Uncama had time to throw his spear.

Uncama could run like the wind and he gave chase. When the animal reached the river it ran into a deep hole at the water's edge. Uncama was a brave, and bold hunter. He didn't hesitate. He followed the animal into the hole and came to an underground country. The animal disappeared and Uncama found himself in a village amongst a tribe of savage dwarfs who attacked him.

94

Uncama barely escaped with his life. He ran back the way he had come followed by a hail of spears.

When he returned to the village no one seemed to recognize him. Uncama could see no one he knew either.

"Where are my friends?" he asked. "And where is my wife?"

"Which wife would that be?" asked a youth.

"Do not joke. . .the wife of Uncama of course."

"I suppose you mean the Uncama who disappeared many years ago," said the youth, and led him to an old woman, with wrinkled face and bowed shoulders. Standing beside her was a fully grown man. The man was Uncama's son. Uncama thought he had been away for less than an hour. He did not know that an hour in the underground country of the dwarfs was as long as fifty years anywhere else.

The son, who had been a baby in his mother's arms when Uncama left in pursuit of the strange animal, was now older than Uncama himself.

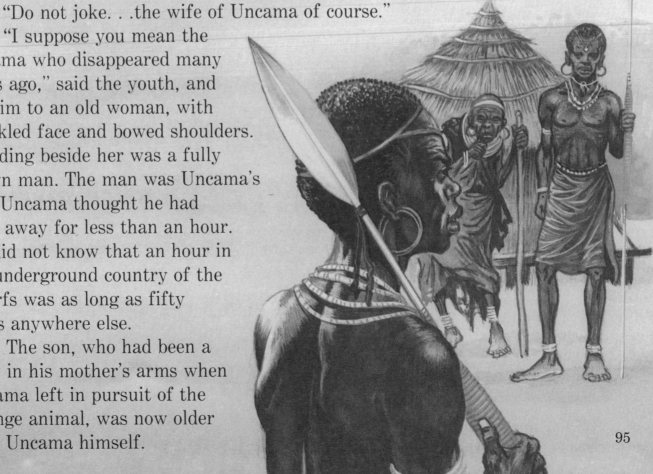

THE CRYSTAL BALL

Once there was an enchantress who had three sons. She did not trust them for she was afraid they would steal her magic powers if they had the chance. She changed the eldest into an eagle and sent him to live in the rocky mountains. His brothers often saw him soaring amongst the clouds. She changed the second into a whale. He was condemned to live in the sea.

When Richard, the youngest of her sons, saw what she had done to his brothers he ran away before she could cast a spell on him.

He had many adventures, and then one day he heard about a king's daughter who was imprisoned in the Castle of the Golden Sun. Several brave men had tried to rescue her but they had all perished. Richard was brave, even though he had run away from his mother's magic, and he decided he would try to rescue the princess himself.

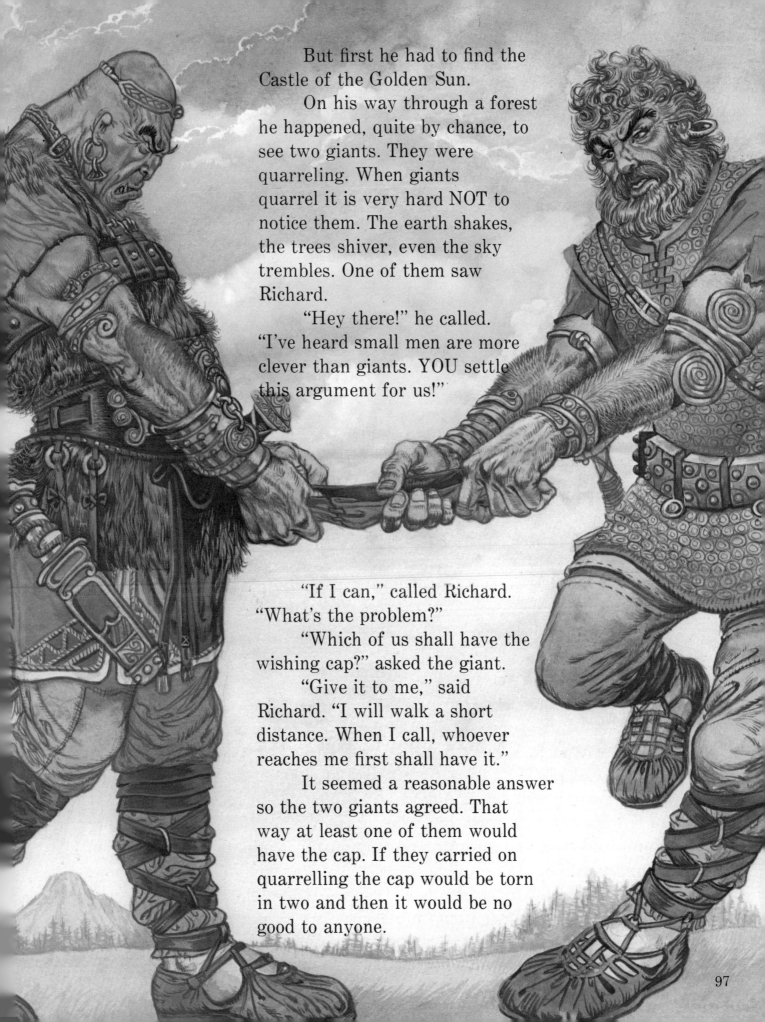

But first he had to find the Castle of the Golden Sun.

On his way through a forest he happened, quite by chance, to see two giants. They were quarreling. When giants quarrel it is very hard NOT to notice them. The earth shakes, the trees shiver, even the sky trembles. One of them saw Richard.

"Hey there!" he called. "I've heard small men are more clever than giants. YOU settle this argument for us!"

"If I can," called Richard. "What's the problem?"

"Which of us shall have the wishing cap?" asked the giant.

"Give it to me," said Richard. "I will walk a short distance. When I call, whoever reaches me first shall have it."

It seemed a reasonable answer so the two giants agreed. That way at least one of them would have the cap. If they carried on quarrelling the cap would be torn in two and then it would be no good to anyone.

Richard put the cap on his own head and began to walk, but he was so busy thinking his own thoughts he forgot to call out to the giants. "Ah," he sighed, "if only I could find the Castle of the Golden Sun." No sooner had he spoken than he was standing outside the castle gates. The wishing cap really was a proper wishing cap.

Richard found the king's daughter in a room deep in the heart of the castle. He couldn't help gasping when he saw her. She was SO wrinkled, and SO ugly, he wanted to turn his head away.

"This is not my real form," said the princess. "I have been bewitched. You may see how I really appear in the mirror, for a mirror cannot lie." The princess looked into her hand mirror so that Richard could see her reflection. She was very beautiful.

"How can the spell be broken?" asked Richard.

"He who holds the crystal ball in front of the Enchanter will destroy his power and I will become myself again," said the princess.

"Where can I find the crystal ball?" asked Richard.

"You must kill the wild bull that lives at the foot of the mountain. From it will spring a fiery bird which has in its body a red hot egg. The crystal ball lies in the yolk of the egg. You must make the bird drop the egg, but if it falls to the ground it will burn everything near it, and the egg and the crystal ball will melt. If that happens then the spell will never be broken." A tear fell onto her cheek.

"Do not cry," said Richard.

He found the bull exactly where the princess said he would.
He killed the bull as the princess said he must and from its
body rose the fiery bird. It rose into the sky and was about to
disappear into the mountains when an eagle appeared. It was
Richard's own brother in his enchanted form. As Richard watched,
the eagle chased the fiery bird towards the sea. They were
almost at the waters edge when the fiery bird dropped the egg.

It fell onto the roof of a fisherman's hut standing on the shore. Flames leapt from the thatch. Smoke billowed into the sky. Soon the egg, and the crystal ball it carried, would be melted in the heat

Just as Richard thought all was lost, a whale, Richard's second enchanted brother, swam close to the shore and caused a great wave to swell up over the beach. The rush of water swept right over the hut and put out the fire.

Richard searched in the wet
ashes until he found the egg.
The cold sea water had cooled it
so quickly the shell had cracked.
Richard peeled away the broken
pieces and found the crystal
ball inside, quite unharmed.

The Enchanter shuddered when he saw Richard had the crystal
ball.

"My power has gone," he said. "YOU are now the King of
the Castle of the Golden Sun." Then he left the castle never to
return.

Richard married the king's daughter and with the crystal
ball restored his two brothers to their rightful shape. They
all lived happily ever after, in the Castle of the Golden Sun.

MOTHER HOLLE

Once there were two step-sisters, who were as different as chalk and cheese. Martha was idle and never did a thing unless she HAD to, which wasn't very often for she was her mother's favourite. Anna was always busy. She HAD to be, for she was only a step-daughter.

One day, Anna was sitting in the garden spinning when she pricked her finger. A speck of blood fell onto the shuttle. She was trying to wash it clean when it slipped from her fingers and fell to the bottom of the well.

"YOU dropped it! YOU must go down and get it!" shouted her step-mother in such a rage that Anna had no choice but to do as she was told. She must have bumped her head as she fell, for she remembered nothing until she woke, and found herself in a pleasant field. She got to her feet and began to walk. Presently she came to an oven.

"Take me out . . . before I burn," cried the bread in the oven.

Anna took the bread from the oven and set it to cool.

A little further on she came to a tree.

"Shake me!" cried the tree. "My apples are ripe!"

Anna shook the tree. When all the apples had fallen she piled them neatly, then went on her way until she came to the house of a witch.

"You must come and work for me," said the witch. "Your most important task will be to shake my feather bed every morning. I am Mother Holle. If my bed is not shaken properly there will be no snow."

Mother Holle was very kind to Anna and for a while Anna was happy, but then she began to feel homesick.

"You have worked very hard," said Mother Holle, "and I will show you the way home." She took Anna to a hidden door. "Go through," said Mother Holle, handing her the lost shuttle. As Anna stepped through the door a shower of golden rain fell all about her and clung to her hair and her clothes.

"The gold is yours," said Mother Holle. "Goodbye my dear."

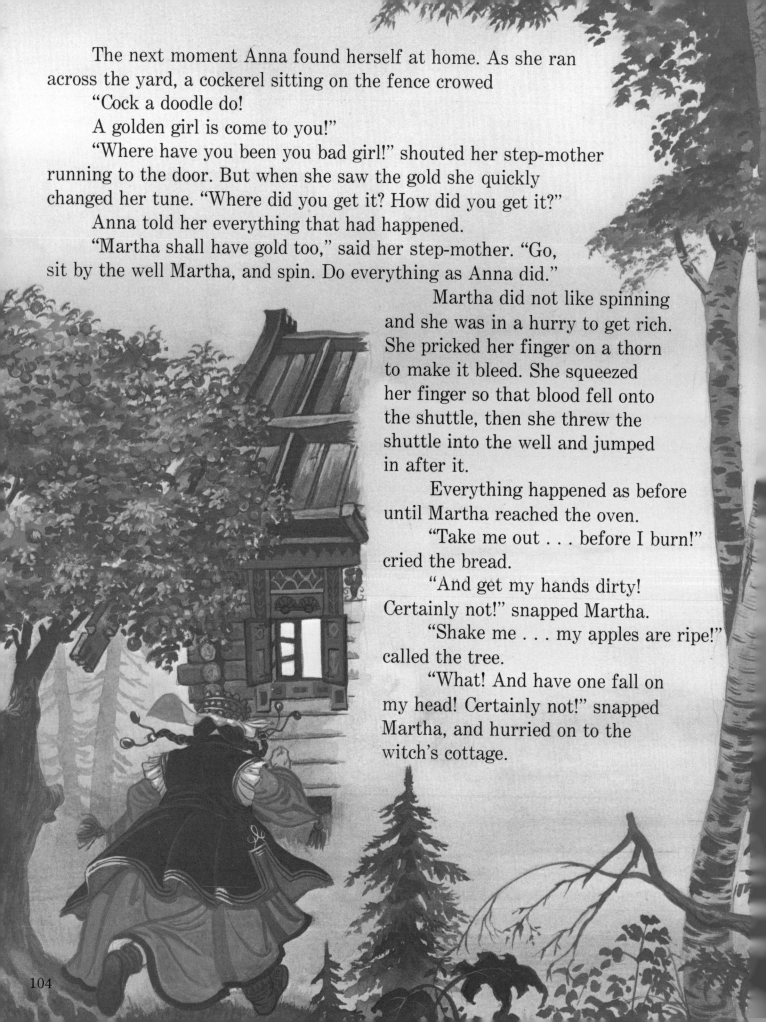

The next moment Anna found herself at home. As she ran across the yard, a cockerel sitting on the fence crowed

"Cock a doodle do!

A golden girl is come to you!"

"Where have you been you bad girl!" shouted her step-mother running to the door. But when she saw the gold she quickly changed her tune. "Where did you get it? How did you get it?"

Anna told her everything that had happened.

"Martha shall have gold too," said her step-mother. "Go, sit by the well Martha, and spin. Do everything as Anna did."

Martha did not like spinning and she was in a hurry to get rich. She pricked her finger on a thorn to make it bleed. She squeezed her finger so that blood fell onto the shuttle, then she threw the shuttle into the well and jumped in after it.

Everything happened as before until Martha reached the oven.

"Take me out . . . before I burn!" cried the bread.

"And get my hands dirty! Certainly not!" snapped Martha.

"Shake me . . . my apples are ripe!" called the tree.

"What! And have one fall on my head! Certainly not!" snapped Martha, and hurried on to the witch's cottage.

"I will come and work for you," she said to Mother Holle, without waiting to be asked.

On the first day she worked well. On the second day she swept the dust under the hearth-rug and didn't bother to shake Mother Holle's mattress at all. On the third day she stayed in bed until mid-afternoon.

"It is time for you to go home," said Mother Holle.

"You must pay me first," said Martha greedily.

"Certainly, I will pay you," said Mother Holle, and led her to the hidden door. This time, instead of a shower of gold descending like rain, a shower of black pitch came pouring down. It covered Martha from head to foot. It was horrid!

"That is just payment for the work you have done," said Mother Holle sternly, and closed the door behind her.

When Martha ran sobbing across the yard to the house, the cockerel sitting on the fence crowed,

"Cock a doodle do!

A dirty girl is come to you!"

105

NILS IN THE FOREST
(A Danish story)

Nils had spent the morning gathering firewood in the forest. When his sack was full with dry twigs he sat down under a tree, and took out his dinner. He had just unwrapped his bread and was about to take a bite from his cheese when a tiny dwarf with a long yellow beard appeared from nowhere and stood in front of him.

"Spare a coin so that a hungry old man can buy food," said the dwarf, holding out his wrinkled hand.

"I'm sorry," said Nils, "I have no coins, but I will gladly share my bread and cheese with you." And without waiting for the dwarf to reply he gave him half of what he had.

The dwarf ate hungrily and didn't leave a crumb. When he had finished Nils handed him his flask. "Wash it down with some ale," he said.

The dwarf drank exactly half, no more and no less, and handed the flask back to Nils. Then, without warning, he clapped his hands and disappeared as suddenly as he had appeared.

"Well I never," said Nils, when he had got over his surprise. "And not even a thank you for eating half my dinner."

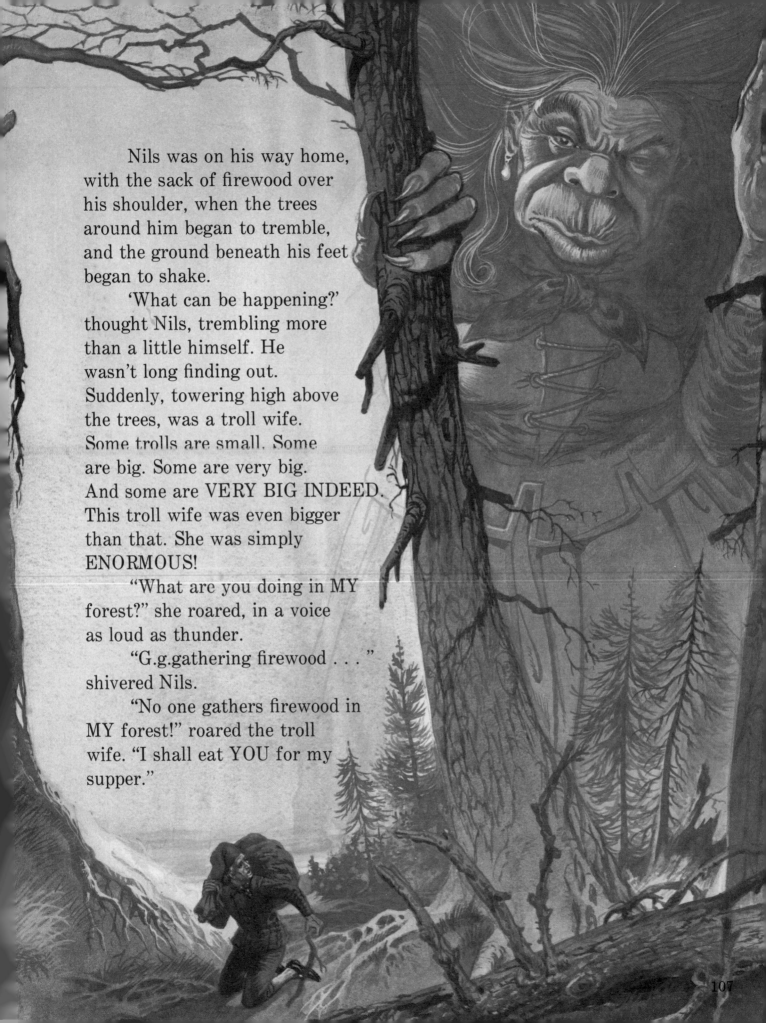

Nils was on his way home, with the sack of firewood over his shoulder, when the trees around him began to tremble, and the ground beneath his feet began to shake.

'What can be happening?' thought Nils, trembling more than a little himself. He wasn't long finding out. Suddenly, towering high above the trees, was a troll wife. Some trolls are small. Some are big. Some are very big. And some are VERY BIG INDEED. This troll wife was even bigger than that. She was simply ENORMOUS!

"What are you doing in MY forest?" she roared, in a voice as loud as thunder.

"G.g.gathering firewood . . ." shivered Nils.

"No one gathers firewood in MY forest!" roared the troll wife. "I shall eat YOU for my supper."

"Please . . . don't do that. I have a wife and seven children at home. How will they live without me to look after them?"

The troll wife was in a playful mood. "Run and hide," she said, "and I will come and look for you. The first time I find you I will let you go. The second time I find you I will also let you go. But the third time I find you I shall EAT YOU . . . now off with you . . . run and hide!"

Nils dashed here, there, and everywhere in a panic. How could he hide from a troll wife? It was impossible. He had almost given up hope of escaping alive when the dwarf with the long yellow beard re-appeared.

"Do not worry," said the dwarf. "I will hide you." And taking his axe he chopped a splinter from a tree trunk. "In you go," he said. He pushed Nils into the space left by the splinter, then put the splinter back on top of him.

"She will never find you in there," laughed the dwarf.

He laughed too soon. When
the troll wife came looking for
Nils she was carrying an axe.

"Where are you going?"
asked the dwarf.

"To cut down a tree, of
course," said the troll wife.
And she cut down the very tree
in which Nils was hiding.

"Found you!" she said as
she pulled him out. "Run and
hide again," she said as she
put him on the ground.

"Come with me," whispered the dwarf. He led Nils out of
the forest and to the side of a lake where there were thick reed
beds. He tapped Nils on the shoulder and Nils shrank to the
size of a pin. Then the dwarf took a reed, broke it in two,
put Nils inside the hollow stem, put the two halves of reed
together, and put the reed back into the reed bed.

"She will NEVER find you in there," laughed the dwarf.

"Where are you going?" he asked, as the troll wife came up
behind him with a sharp knife.

"Where do you think? To cut reeds of course." And with
one big swish, she had cut them all.

"Found you!" she laughed, as she shook the reeds and Nils tumbled to the ground. "Now run and hide once more. Next time I find you I shall put you in my cooking pot."

Nils was in despair.

"Worry not," said the dwarf. "We'll outwit her yet." He dipped his hand into the lake and caught a fish. He broke it in two and placed Nils inside it. Then he joined the two halves together and threw the fish back into the lake. It swam away with a quick wiggle of its tail, and with Nils safe inside.

When the troll wife came looking for Nils she was carrying a wash tub and a fishing net.

"Where are you going?" asked the dwarf.

"To catch a fish for my supper of course," she laughed.

She pushed the wash tub into the water and climbed into it herself. She paddled with her hands until she was in the middle of the lake, then she took her fishing net and dipped it into the smooth, calm water.

"I can see the VERY fish I am looking for," she called.

The dwarf, who was watching from the shore, bent close to the waters edge and began to blow. He blew and he blew and he BLEW. What a storm he blew up. The wind howled! The thunder roared! The smooth lake became a raging sea. The waves grew higher, and rougher and rougher. The wash tub pitched, and turned and tumbled.

"Mercy! Mercy!" screamed the troll wife, clinging desperately to the sides of the wash tub.

"If you have ever shown mercy, then mercy will be shown to you," said the dwarf. Instantly, the wash tub overturned and tipped the troll wife into the lake. She was so heavy she sank straight to the bottom and was never seen again.

As soon as the dwarf was sure she was gone for good he stopped blowing and the lake became as calm as a puddle. He caught the fish, broke it open, took Nils out and restored him to his proper size. Then he put the fish together again and threw it into the lake. It swam away with a merry swish of its tail and without a backward glance.

The dwarf took Nils to the cave where the troll wife had lived. It was full of gold.

"Take it," said the dwarf. "It is all yours."

"Thank you . . . " gasped Nils.

"And thank you for the dinner you so kindly shared with me," said the dwarf. And with that he clapped his hands and vanished.

Nils never saw the dwarf again, but there was never a day which passed when he did not think of him, and the strange adventures that followed his appearance.

THE BOASTFUL TAILOR

One day, a tailor who was always boasting about how clever he was, decided to go out and see something of the world. He walked a long way and at last came to a steep hill behind which he could see the tops of some trees, and a very tall tower. The tower was so tall it disappeared into a cloud.

"I'll go and see who lives there," said the tailor boldly. "I am afraid of nothing." He even boasted to himself.

He had only gone a few yards when something odd happened. The tower began to move. The tailor rubbed his eyes. Surely he must be imagining it? Towers don't move. But this one did. It stepped right over the hill and stood in front of the tailor. It wasn't a tower at all. It was a leg. A giant's leg. It was quickly followed by a second. And where there are two giant legs, there is bound to be a giant.

113

"WHAT DO YOU WANT?" bellowed the giant.

The tailor put his cupped hands to his mouth and called back, "I want to earn myself a crust of bread!"

"You may come and work for me," bellowed the giant. The tailor didn't think it was an offer he could very well refuse, since he was so small and the giant was so big.

"What wage will you give me?" he asked.

"I will give you three hundred and sixty five days every year, and an extra day every leap year," said the giant.

"That sounds fair," said the tailor, determined however, to make his escape as quickly as he could.

The first task the giant set him was to fetch water.

"Will one jugful be enough?" asked the tailor. "Or shall I bring the well? If the well isn't enough I will bring the spring too."

"No, no, the jug holds enough," said the giant. And he thought to himself. 'This is no ordinary man if he can fetch a well and a spring too. I must be careful what I say to him.'

The second task the giant set the tailor was to cut wood.

"Why not let me bring the whole forest and be done with it," said the tailor boastfully.

"No, no, there's no need to do that," growled the giant into his beard. "Fetch well and spring too . . . cut a whole forest! What sort of man is this?"

The third task the giant set the tailor was to shoot two wild pigs for their supper.

"I'll bring you a thousand," boasted the tailor.

"No, no, two will do," said the giant. And he muttered into his beard, "Fetch well and spring too . . . cut a whole forest . . . bring a thousand pigs. This man is dangerous. The sooner I am rid of him the better." He was so worried he lay awake all night trying to think of a way to get rid of the tailor.

The next morning the giant took the tailor to a marsh where willow trees grew. The giant picked up the tailor and sat him on one of the springy willow branches.

"I don't suppose even YOU can bend that branch to the ground," said the giant.

"Oh yes I can!" boasted the tailor. He took a deep breath and held it inside his chest, then he pushed at the branch. Slowly it began to bend.

"More . . ." said the giant.

The tailor pressed harder. The branch sank lower. The tailor's breath had disappeared. He needed to take a new one. He HAD to take a new one. But the instant he opened his mouth to breathe in, the springy willow branch hurled him into the air, like a catapult hurling a stone. Higher he went . . . higher and higher. He must have gone over the moon because he was never seen again, much to the giant's relief.

If the tailor hadn't been so boastful, he would probably be sitting at home now, telling his grandchildren about a giant he had once known.

THE SPIRIT IN THE BOTTLE

Once there was a woodcutter who worked and saved all he could so that he could send his son William to school. But times were hard and the day came when all the money he had saved was spent and his son had to return home.

"Do not worry, Father," said William. "I will come into the forest with you and help you cut wood. We will be able to earn enough to keep ourselves."

"How can you help me?" sighed the woodcutter. "You are not used to such work . . .besides, I've only one axe. We are far too poor to buy another."

"We'll ask our neighbour to lend us one of his until I can earn enough to buy one of my own," said William.

The next day they went into the forest together. William was young and the work was new to him. He enjoyed every minute of it, and whistled and sang as merrily as any bird.

At midday the woodcutter said, "Time to rest."

"I'm not a bit tired," said William. So while his father sat under a tree and dozed, he went in search of birds' nests.

117

William climbed trees, looked in bushes and spied on birds sitting in their nests without disturbing any of them. He was looking for a way to climb into the branches of an ancient oak when he heard a voice calling, "Let me out! Let me out!"

"Where are you? Who are you?" called William, looking about and seeing no one.

"I'm at the foot of the tree," answered the voice. "Please let me out."

William poked about amongst the grass and dried leaves, and found a dirty glass bottle lying between two gnarled roots. He rubbed it clean on his sleeve. Sitting hunched inside it, with its knees under its chin was a tiny frog like creature.

"Hallo!" said William. "What are you doing in there?"

"Let me out and I'll tell you," it shouted, banging on the side of the bottle with its tiny fist.

William took out the cork. The little creature shot from the bottle like an arrow and grew and grew and grew, until it was twice as big as William himself.

'I've made a mistake here,' thought William, trembling like a leaf, but trying to keep his wits about him. 'That's a magic spirit if ever I saw one.'

"I was put into that bottle as a punishment," said the spirit. And now you must be punished for letting me out. I am going to kill you."

"I wouldn't have let you out if I'd known then what I know now," said William under his breath. "Hold on! Wait a minute!" he said aloud, as the spirit reached towards him. "How do I know you are who you say you are? I don't see how someone as big as you are could possibly have come from that tiny bottle."

"Oh, don't you!" said the spirit. "Then I'll prove to you that I did." Whereupon he shrank to his former size and crawled back into the bottle.

"Got you!" shouted William and pushed the cork in.

"Let me out!" shouted the spirit in a fury. "LET ME OUT!"

"I'm not silly," said William. "If I let you out you will kill me."

"No I won't . . . I promise I won't," said the spirit. "Please, let me out."

William knew he was taking a risk, but he decided to chance his luck. He held the bottle at arm's length and took out the cork. The spirit was so grateful to be free again it gave William a piece of cloth that had the power to heal any wound, and turn iron and steel into silver.

When William returned his father said crossly,

"You will be far too tired to work this afternoon."

"I'm not tired at all," said William, and secretly rubbed the axe with the magic cloth. It turned the blade to silver, but silver isn't sharp like steel and the first blow he struck with it turned the edge up.

"Now look what you have done you foolish boy!" cried his father. "You have damaged our neighbour's axe. Now I shall have to pay for a new one."

When they got home William said he would ask the blacksmith if the axe could be repaired, but instead of going to the blacksmith he went to the silversmith. The silversmith gave him a small bag of gold in exchange for the axe.

When William next saw his father, he said, "Ask our neighbour how much he will take for his axe."

"I already have," sighed his father. "It's more than I have."

"Give him twice what he asks," said William, and showed his father the bag of gold.

And then, William told his father about the bottle he had found in the wood and the gift the spirit had given him. From that day, William and his father lived in comfort and because William used the magic cloth wisely, he became a very famous doctor.